'I've Decided Your Fate.'

He was so close, his lips nearly brushed hers. The clean familiar scent of him tantalized and beguiled as he took her in his arms.

'This,' he whispered as his lips touched hers.

He meant to keep it brief. But something in her, the soft yielding of her mouth, drew him nearer, holding him closer. She was too sweet. Dear heaven!

The beat of his heart roughened in answer to the enchanting pleasure of her yielding, his kiss deepening, even as his mind said no. Slowly his mouth gentled on hers, and slowly drew away. Looking down at her, he knew he wanted her more than anything. But she was too vulnerable, her emotion in her shadowed eyes too naked.

'One day,' he said with a tenderness he'd never known was in him. 'But not this day."

Dear Reader,

The celebration of Silhouette Desire's® 15th Anniversary continues this month! First there's a wonderful treat in store for you as Ann Major brings us the next story in her fantastic CHILDREN OF DESTINY series with June's MAN OF THE MONTH, *Nobody's Child*. And Elizabeth August spins a stirring tale in *The Bridal Shower*, the second book in the ALWAYS A BRIDESMAID! mini-series. The third is in Silhouette Sensation®, next month.

Journey's End is the latest instalment in BJ James's popular BLACK WATCH series—stories of men and women who've sworn to live—and love—by a code of honour. There's also the third and final story in Peggy Moreland's WIVES WANTED! mini-series, entitled *Lone Star Kind of Man*.

This month's wonderful line-up is completed with delicious love stories by Lass Small and Judith McWilliams. And next month, look for six more wonderful Silhouette Desire books, including a Tallchief MAN OF THE MONTH by Cait London!

Desire™...it's the name you can trust for dramatic, sensuous, engrossing stories written by your bestselling favourites and terrific newcomers. So read and enjoy!

The Editors

Journey's End

BJ JAMES

SILHOUETTE
Desire®

*Silhouette, Silhouette Desire and Colophon
are registered trademarks of Harlequin Books S.A.,
used under licence.*

*First published in Great Britain 1998
Silhouette Books, Eton House, 18-24 Paradise Road,
Richmond, Surrey TW9 1SR*

© BJ James 1997

ISBN 0 373 76106 6

22-9806

*Printed and bound in Great Britain
by Mackays of Chatham PLC, Chatham*

BJ JAMES

married her school sweetheart straight out of college and soon found that books were delightful companions during her lonely nights as a doctor's wife. But she never dreamed she would be more than a reader, never expected to be one of the blessed, letting her imagination soar, weaving magic of her own.

Other novels by BJ James

Silhouette Desire®

The Sound of Goodbye
~~Twice in a Lifetime~~
Shiloh's Promise
Winter Morning
Slade's Woman
A Step Away
Tears of the Rose
The Man with the Midnight Eyes
Pride and Promises
Another Time, Another Place
The Hand of an Angel
*Heart of the Hunter
*The Saint of Bourbon Street
*A Wolf in the Desert
†Whispers in the Dark

Silhouette Sensation®

~~Broken Spurs~~

*Men of the Black Watch
†The Black Watch

FORWARD

In desperate answer to a need prompted by changing times and mores, Simon McKinzie, dedicated and uncompromising leader of The Black Watch, has been called upon by the president of the United States to form a more covert and more dangerous division of his most clandestine clan. Ranging the world in ongoing assembly of this unique unit, he has gathered and will gather in the elite among the elite—those born with the gift or the curse of skills transcending the norm. Men and women who bring extraordinary and uncommon talents in answer to extraordinary and uncommon demands.

They are, in most cases, men and women who have plummeted to the brink of hell because of their talents. Tortured souls who have stared down into the maw of destruction, been burned by its fires, yet have come back, better, surer, stronger. Driven and Colder.

As officially nameless as The Black Watch, to those few who have had the misfortune and need of calling on their dark service, they are known as Simon's chosen... Simon's marauders.

Prologue

"**No!**"

Boot heels thudding on the bare wood floor, Ty O'Hara scowled and paced and listened.

"No," he declared again into the telephone. "There have been guests here from early spring into early August. I can't have any over the winter. I won't."

In rare impatience, he whipped his Stetson from his head, sailing it across the room. Any other time he would have been mildly pleased when he scored a bull's-eye, with the stained and worn hat settling perfectly onto the peg by the door. Another time, but not today. Not when he had the sinking, drowning feeling he was waging a losing battle.

"I said no. N, period. O, period. A short, simple word an intelligent woman such as yourself should have no trouble comprehending."

He stopped his pacing abruptly, his fingers raked through sweat flattened hair. "Of course I love you. Of course I trust you. Of course I know what you're asking is exactly the sort of thing that saved you. And of course I know you wouldn't ask unless this was of the direst importance.

"But," he turned to face a bank of windows and the mountainous vista they offered, "the answer is still no."

He found no pleasure in the view. None in his refusal. Sighing, he grumbled, "You don't know what you're asking."

There was silence in the cabin, then, interrupting the coaxing voice whispering in his ear, he demanded, "Why? Why is it so important this Santiago comes here? With the resources Simon McKinzie has at his command, why send his walking wounded to me?"

Finding no resolution in the mountains, Ty turned his back on them. "It was your suggestion?" Closing his eyes he thought of a much loved face with a stubborn chin framed by a wealth of hair only a shade lighter than his own black mane. Of a level gaze a shade darker, descending from deep blue to navy in solemn resolve. Of a mouth that trembled in tender-hearted concern. "Because this is your friend, you promised I would help?"

He began to pace again. "No, I wouldn't want you to break your promise. Yes, I remember our promise to each other. We *are* blood brothers and sisters, Val. We were born that way," he reminded drolly. "No, I haven't forgotten cutting our palms when you were eight and I was ten, then bleeding all over each other to make the bond stronger."

Once he would have smiled at the memory: The five of them, descending in age by one year or two from Devlin, to Kieran, to himself, then Valentina and the youngest, Patience. Five O'Haras huddled together on a summer day, swearing secret and eternal fidelity, biting back pain, dripping O'Hara blood.

A kid's stunt and Dev's idea, but Tynan had decided more than once over the years that the ritual had succeeded. Why else had he always been such a soft touch for his sisters? Why now, he wondered as he went down in flames. Crashing, burning, sighing in defeat, he agreed, "All right."

Pausing, he waited for the long distance jubilation to subside. "That's what I said. Yes, I promise." His brows plummeted in a deepening frown. "When? When will this Merrill Santiago come?"

Gripping the telephone, he squinted and nodded. "You were so certain I would agree, he's already on his way?"

"She?"

His eyes blinked open, the telephone crackled under his grasp. "She! Tell me this is a joke, Val. I need for you to tell me this is a joke."

The open phone line hummed hollowly in his ear.

"Val! No! Don't you dare."

With the sounding of a pleased and wicked chuckle, the line went dead. Valentina had seized her victory and signed off. Leaving her brother with a broken connection and a growing sense of dismay.

"A woman!" Ty muttered to the four walls, to the mountains, to the darkening Montana sky. "Merrill Santiago is a woman." The receiver clattered into its cradle. "What the hell have you done? Why, Valentina?"

Brooding in the gathering of twilight, Tynan knew with dreadful certainty there was no help for his sister's coup. No remedy for an O'Hara fait accompli.

"Caged with a wounded kitten for the winter. A female kitten! God help me. God help us both." Teeth clenched, he scowled into the first fall of night. "Beginning with tomorrow."

One

Snow!

Tynan O'Hara looked into a cloudless Montana sky and offered another silent plea. He cajoled. He implored. Before that he'd commanded, demanded. And he'd cursed.

But Mother Nature, that fickle and wily lady, hadn't listened. No more than Valentina had listened.

"When will I learn to say no, and mean it?" he asked the wolf sitting patiently at his feet.

As it echoed through the comfortable, but spartan room, the sound of his deep voice would have been startling if there had been ears other than his own and the wolf's to hear. He spoke softly for a man so large, his words filled with unshakable, ironic calm even in anger. Anger directed at himself, destined to be short lived as his anger always was.

Leaving the window and its ever changing view, he crossed to a woodstove. The scarred and monstrously ugly antique, more than thrice his thirty-five years, had proven more than thrice as practical for his needs than one less ugly and more

modern. Lifting a battered tin pot from the iron top, he refilled
a tin cup nearly as battered. Sipping the brew that would have
grown hair on his chest if it weren't there already, he returned
to his study of sprawling pastures and silent mountains. The
latter, riddled with deep gashes of chasms carved by the great
rivers of ice called down by the unheeding Mother Nature
aeons before, forever fascinating.

Ty moved with an easy grace, walked with an agile step.
Attentive and poised as he was in everything.

Given his manner, his coal black hair, his chiseled cheeks
and darkly weathered skin, were it not for his eyes, he might
have been mistaken for a member of the nearby Indian tribe.
But as there were no ears to hear the soft, deep voice, neither
were there eyes to see the eyes that were as blue as a Montana
lake, bluer than its sky. Irish eyes, an arresting reminder of
his black Irish heritage, in a thoroughly American face.

The quietude with which he surrounded himself, with which
he unfailingly reacted, told less of his share of the fabled Irish
temper than of a remarkable control. Which, now, as he looked
out over the rugged land, was sorely tested.

This was his home, his time. The season of the tourist, the
interim when he served as guide and outfitter for the temporary
guest, was over. The season purposely cut short, with most of
the horses moved to more temperate pastures; the summer
hands decamped, scattered, taking up their winter's work.

And Tynan O'Hara had returned to the small cabin no tourist and few ranch hands had ever entered.

He wasn't misanthropic. Far from it. He truly enjoyed these
people he called summer folk, enchanting the ladies with his
easygoing charm, engaging the gentlemen with his down-to-
earth approach to life and living. And all of it easily, naturally
done, with Ty hardly realizing that he had. He was always
glad to see them come, the wide-eyed and eager adventurers
with childhood dreams of the West tucked in their hearts and
shining on their faces. He delighted in sharing with them this
land, the land that had chosen him, the wilderness that fulfilled
his own dream and halted his restless wandering.

Yet when summer was done, and the mildest of autumn past, he was equally as glad to see them go. As delighted to have the land he called *Fini Terre* to himself once again.

Now winter loomed and, with no respect for the calendar, could arrive at any minute. When it came, born on westerly winds created by the ever changing Pacific Coast weather, like all survivors of this challenging parcel of earth, he would be ready.

In a barn divided into both stable and garage, there was a truck, a snowmobile, and a snowplow. Stored in sheds set apart were gasoline and hay to fuel whatever form of transportation he wished or would need.

A plentiful supply of wood was chopped, split and stacked in a shed attached to the small cabin. An ample reserve of food and medical supplies had been laid down in the cellar, along with a selection of his favorite wines. Just in case, though he didn't know *what* case, there were kegs of water, as well. In this place of clean streams, lakes, and snow, it required a stretch of the imagination to envision the lack of water becoming a problem. Within the cabin, itself, there were lamps and oil, candles, and books. Even snowshoes and skis, and every other conceivable supply, from flashlights to extra buttons.

As efficiently as the ever busy red squirrel, he had prepared. And like an old bear he looked forward to the six foot snows and was ready to hibernate. Like an old bear in a tuxedo, he admitted ruefully when he thought of the generator, waiting and ready for when the electricity would inevitably fail; the sophisticated radio he would use only in the event of an emergency; and a state-of-the-art computer residing in the small, anterior room off the gallery that he called his lair.

"What the hell happens now when the snows cover the windows and seal the doors?" he asked the wolf as he regarded a sky that showed no sign of granting the very weather of which he spoke. "What will I do when the electricity stops and the generator dies, and the lonelies creep in?"

The lonelies.

His name for a very integral part of living as he did. That endless interval when Spring is nearly a dream realized, yet Winter lingers arrogantly, behaving its worst, its mood most capricious. A condition perfect for sending one plummeting into depression and the madness of cabin fever, or for strengthening one's resolve and renewing one's soul as it did for Ty.

"What will it do to Simon McKinzie's walking wounded? What miracle does he expect of me?"

The wolf grinned, thumped his tail once on the bare floor, and kept his own counsel. Tilting his head, he presented the soft, vulnerable underside of his ebony throat to be scratched.

"No answer, huh?" Without interrupting his vigil, Ty stroked the wolf. "I guess you're thinking it's my own fault, that we wouldn't be in this predicament if I'd only said no to Valentina. But could you say no to your sister? Wait!" In a forestalling motion he lifted his hand from the wolf's throat. "Don't tell me, I know. But I promise you, sport, you'd be as big a sucker as I've always been if your sisters *were* like Val. Or Patience."

The wolf turned an uncertain look at him.

"You don't think so, I take it?" A nearly silent rumble drew taut the furry black throat as the wolf turned to stare again out the window. "Better think again. You'd understand if you knew their history with me. No," he corrected. "You'd understand better if you knew my slavish history with them."

With a self mocking shake of his head, Tynan O'Hara murmured, "I keep telling myself the day will come when I won't be such an easy mark for either of my sisters. But, in my heart, I know that will also be the proverbial cold day in Hell."

The rumble became a soft growl, as the wolf grew uncommonly impatient with his master's uncommon monologue.

"I know, sport," he soothed the wolf. "I'm not completely blinded, I see it, too."

A flash of light where there should be only grass and rolling hills had caught human as well as canine attention. Setting the cup aside, with hands shoved abruptly into the hip pockets of his jeans, his mouth drawn into a stark line and eyes narrowed against the brilliant unsullied sky, Ty waited with the wolf for a second flash.

"There," he muttered. A sound not unlike a growl itself.

As if needing only this cue, the wolf drew himself to attention. Ears perked and acutely tuned. Eyes, no less blue than any fourth generation Irishman's, riveted. As the ridge of fur bristled the length of his spine, he stood like a shadowy sentinel by the side of the human he'd chosen as his own.

The light flashed, then again in another place, drawing ever closer to the cabin. "And there," Ty confirmed grimly. "Coming too fast."

The flash, light glinting off the windshield of a vehicle approaching as if it expressed the turbulent mood of its driver, became constant. In a matter of minutes, if it made the grade that dipped, then rose to the cabin, the Land Rover would be in his yard.

The vexing winter boarder would have arrived.

"Easy, easy," Ty said as much to himself as the wolf. A plume of dust heralded the threatened advent. Sighing, he groused again under his breath, "It looks like there will be three of us for the winter after all."

Curious at the strange mood of his human, or perhaps in commiseration, the wolf nipped gently at the corded seam of Ty's jeans.

"Are you wondering why I don't stop grumbling and live up to my word?" In a stroke of his finger under the animal's throat, Ty lifted its gaze to his. "Are you thinking a promise is a promise, especially to Valentina? Is that it? Well, you're right. So, I suppose we'd best go make like a welcoming committee."

With the wolf at his heels, he stepped to the door and opened it. At the edge of the porch he paused, breathing in deeply, savoring what he feared might be his last comfortable breath for a while. "Just one more question, Shadow." He addressed the wolf by its name for the first time. "What the hell are we going to do with a woman in our all male sanctum for eight long, cold months?"

The wolf gave him another slow, considering look.

Lifting a sardonic brow, Ty laughed, "Spare me the 'if you don't know, Buster, I'm not going to tell you' looks. Believe me, that's a complication I don't need and don't want."

The wolf only looked at him, silent and still, hackles at half mast.

"If we're lucky, maybe she'll hate us on sight. Hopefully, in time to hightail it back to the train crossing tonight and the airport tomorrow."

Descending the steps, man and wolf crossed the small lawn. At the edge of the drive they waited. With no appreciable sign of caution, the approaching vehicle disappeared into the declension that set Tynan O'Hara's world apart. "There's still hope, Shadow. Until the very last, there's hope. Who knows?" Ty shrugged heavy shoulders clad in a dark woolen shirt. "Maybe two ugly guys won't be her idea of winter companions."

The Land Rover topped the rise, skidded to a halt, obscuring car and driver in a cloud of dust. A shower of loose stone pelted Ty's shins and boots. The wolf took a discreet step back as if disassociating himself from the man as much as avoiding the flying debris, Ty coughed and blinked, observing the desertion wryly.

"Okay, have it your way, traitor," he said softly, without rancor. "One ugly guy and a conceited mutt."

"A good-looking guy and man's best friend," Merrill Santiago sputtered through clenched teeth as she glared through the sifting haze her protesting tires had created.

"A good-looking guy and a wolf," she reassessed her opinion as the furor of her arrival settled, permitting a better view. "The first probably not an iota different from the latter, when one gets past the mustache of one and the fur coat of the other.

"Just what I need!" Gripping the steering wheel as if it were her lifeline with the world she'd left behind, she shivered in distaste. "A winter in exile, fending off mister wonderful, while his wild beast chews off my leg." Fingertips tapping in a fast paced rhythm that matched her mounting dismay, she exhaled wearily, dispatching a tangle of gold streaked bangs from her eyes.

Instinct and trust in Simon McKinzie warned that she was judging wrongly and unfairly. That there was, no doubt, far more to the character of this man than a craggy and arresting face. Perhaps more than she would want.

Her bleak gaze strayed from man and beast to the land, the essence of wilderness. Depression and the first stirring of angry frustration could not blind her to its far-reaching magnificence. Within the bounds of a single glance lay a panorama of natural beauty. A vast sanctuary hewn by chaos and cataclysm and the simple wearing of the ages. Rugged, diverse, a land pristine and undisturbed. Inhabited by none but wild creatures and stalwart men, as those who waited in uncanny stillness.

Beneath the weight of twin blue gazes, she felt a sudden urge to run, and continue to run. Until those piercing eyes could not touch her, and would never see into the darkness of her soul.

But no. She would not run, would not even walk away. She'd given her word, the last remaining measure of her integrity. In a moment of mental turmoil she had succumbed first to Valentina's gentle persuasion, then to Simon's kind, but implacable coercion, agreeing to this sojourn into the wilderness.

She'd promised to stay...and she would.

"For the winter." A time that seemed to stretch as endlessly before her as the sea of mountains surrounding her. "Only that."

Catching up a small duffel bag she jerked open the door and climbed from the rented Land Rover. Standing stiffly on cramped legs, with her shoulders back and her head up, she tried not to stare at the land, the wolf, and the man. "Tynan O'Hara, I presume."

"Yes, ma'am, presumption right on target," Ty drawled and took a step forward to take her bag. When she refused with an impatient jerk, he smiled and hooked his thumbs in the back pockets of his jeans. Concealing his surprise that the dazzling creature who stood before him bore so little resemblance to the stevedore he expected, he continued in his own imperturbable manner. "Unless you'd taken a wrong turn nearly forty miles back, it would be hard to presume anything else."

"Forty miles!" She stared at him then. "Forty?" In spite of her best efforts, her temper flared. "Do you mean to tell me we're that far from civilization? Just the two of us?"

"I doubt you would call the next ranch civilization exactly." Ty fought back a grin. It was hard not to grin when one was eternally afflicted with attention deficit when it came to anger. And especially when faced with a woman who was, maybe, a fraction more than half his size, twice as angry, and looked as if she'd stepped off the pages of a fairy tale. "But it is that far by public roads, give or take eight or ten miles and a shortcut or two."

"Give or take? Eight or ten?" She shook her head, and curls of many hues of gold tumbled around her shoulders. "In the guise of a strong suggestion, Simon ordered me to Montana for some R and R, and peace and seclusion. He didn't say it would be in the middle of nowhere."

"The middle of paradise."

Merrill was too caught up in her own tumult to notice his correction. "Valentina and Simon said I would be lodging with Valentina's brother. But I didn't expect he would be, ahh...you would be so..." With a fretful frown, she shrugged, a small lift of elegant shoulders. "Let's just say, I expected you would be older. Maybe not an old coot, but still not quite so..." Biting back the word virile, she settled for half truths, "...so young!" Seizing on the word, she belabored the obvious. "I didn't expect you to be so young."

Ty chuckled, and then his laugh spilled out like rich, dark brandy flowing over her. The sound was heady and soothing, and if she'd been in a receptive mood, comforting. "Laugh if you will, Mr. O'Hara. But, frankly, I don't imagine that you're any happier about having me here than I am about being here.''

"Winter boarders are rare.'' And allowing himself to enjoy this first meeting with a beguiling woman was scarcely the same as enduring a winter of confinement with her.

"How rare?'' Merrill persisted, refusing to settle for his noncommittal response. "On a scale of seldom to never, for example.''

"Never.'' Ty was nothing if not honest, and if togetherness was their destiny, he would begin as he intended to be.

Through narrowed eyes, she took his measure, noting the strength in the lean hard body, the calm of his pleasingly rugged face. He had the sophisticated presence of one who had lived hard and fully, and well. And yet, in his prime, he'd chosen solitude. Magnificent solitude, but solitude nevertheless, with only the wolf as his companion. She wondered why.

Curious and intrigued, as she hadn't been for months, she searched the glittering depths of his gaze, seeking, but never finding, the true man beneath the easy charm. At the edge of their space, the wolf lurked, watchful and still, as if waiting to pounce or play. One gorgeous creature as much an enigma as the other.

"Am I to assume, then, that it's usually just you, the wolf, the mountains?'' Her voice was stilted and stiff, as if rusted from disuse. "And, of course, a hundred feet of snow.''

"Three quarters and a half.''

The laconic answer blindsided her, leaving her confounded. "Three quarters and a half? By that do you mean three quarters and a half of a mountain, three quarters and a half of a hundred feet of snow, or...''

"Neither.'' A silent signal brought the wolf to his side. "This is Shadow, he's only three quarters and a half wolf, and just so you'll know, the snow rarely exceeds six feet,'' he drawled. "In all else, you assume correctly.''

"She snookered you, didn't she?''

It was Ty's turn to be blindsided. "Snookered? She?''

Suddenly and for no apparent reason, for the first time in

longer than she could remember, Merrill was enjoying herself. "Wrapped you around her little finger, broad shoulders, stubborn chin and all, I'd bet."

"You think that's possible?"

In this case, Merrill hadn't a doubt. "If it were the right woman. Yes," she nodded thoughtfully. "Most definitely possible."

"And who would you suggest that woman is?"

"Your sister, my colleague and friend. Valentina Courtenay, nee O'Hara."

Ty didn't bother with denials that would seem foolish in the face of events. Shrugging the broad shoulders she'd described, he conceded, "I've never learned to say no to her, and now I've come to the conclusion I never will."

"Let me guess. She let you believe I was a man when she asked that you share your winter refuge."

"Until the last minute."

Merrill laughed, the haunted look faded from her gaze for an instant. "If it's any consolation, I think she only wanted what she considered best for me."

"Peace, respite, isolation."

The remnants of laughter lingered, stealing worry and years from her face. "Good guess."

Ty smiled in response. The tiny quirk of his lips that in summer set the hearts of both big and little girls lurching. "Not much of a stretch, when they are the commodities this part of the country possesses in abundance."

Merrill found her gaze drawn again to the majesty befitting the name he'd given it. *Fini Terre,* a description as much as a definition for a ranch lying on the far northern boundaries of his country. A tribute to its namesake, a plantation as far south, where the O'Haras had spent a happy summer long ago.

"*Fini Terre,* Land's End." A name fraught with hidden meaning for a land of tranquility. Valentina had called it Journey's End. Perhaps it was both, or one in the same, for this man. "More than commodities," she mused. "A gift."

"A gift Val thinks you have need of. Will you let it heal you?"

Temper stirring again in another of the mercuric mood swings that had plagued her for weeks, Merrill reacted caustically. "I said nothing about healing, or needing to be healed."

"No," Ty agreed mildly, "you didn't. But we all need repair, in one degree or another, at some time in our lives. A need even greater when we seek out the solitude of places such as this."

"As you did when you chose the land?"

"The land chose me, claiming me for its own. As, perhaps, it will you, Merrill Santiago." As it had begun already. He saw it in her face, and in her eyes. He had only to look past the seething brew of guilt and resentment to know she was half in love with Montana from the start.

"Perhaps," she ventured, temper mellowing as quickly as it ignited. Sustained anger required too much effort. Sustaining any mood or thought, or expressing any desire required more emotional energy than she had to expend.

"Then you'll stay?" And suddenly, he wanted to give her the peace and the healing Simon and Valentina had sent her to find.

"I would be a less than pleasant companion."

"Then we needn't be companions at all. Neither friends, nor enemies."

"No?" His answer startled her, making her wonder again what manner of man he was that he could make her feel and think as no one else ha⸺ so long. "Sealed away from the world, alone and isolated, underfoot and tripping over each other in a small cabin? Out of human necessity we would become one or the other."

"Not unless we both want it."

"This is insane, you must realize that," she declared, but with little emphasis. "You can't have wanted anyone to disrupt your winter idyll."

"I didn't." The truth, always the truth. The only way Tynan O'Hara knew.

"But now you do." A statement, not a question, of what she heard in his words, in his voice.

"Seems so."

"Why?"

As she faced him, not challenging so much as simply questioning, the mountains at her back had begun to catch the late afternoon sun, framing her with their red glow. He was struck again by her small stature, the slender compact body, the deceptive fragility. She was an agent of The Black Watch. More than that, one of Simon's Marauders, the elite among the elite. Men and women singled out from all over the world, chosen by Simon for their uncanny gifts and uncommon skills. Discreetly recruited, exquisitely trained, informed. Ruthless when necessary. Moral, loyal. Dangerous.

If she was fragile, it was a state of mind, and ultimately a physical condition created out of the very strength it eroded. Fragility out of strength—a paradox. A puzzle that must be solved and resolved before he would know the whole woman. The real woman.

The woman, he realized, he'd wanted to know from first glance. A challenging mystery he couldn't send away.

As his gaze held hers, as blue and piercing as a laser, she didn't look away. There was no nervous disquiet, no restless tension. The bedrock strength still survived, still resisted the grief and anguish of a tormented conscience. But for how long? How long before the one thing that could destroy her, would destroy her?

"You haven't answered my question, Mr. O'Hara," she said with a trace of mockery. "Or can you?"

"Perhaps not completely, Miss Santiago, but in part." The only part that he understood, and was ready to admit. "Why do I want you to stay now, when I didn't before?" His eyes strayed from hers, touching on the shadows of sleeplessness lying beneath them, tracing the paths of new lines of tension.

Shadows, not so dark, and lines, not so deeply ingrained, that they couldn't be erased. In time. If she stayed.

"The reason is simple, and as Val anticipated. Because you aren't who I expected and what I expected. And as she knew I would, because I see the hurt that sent you to me."

"To you?"

"To the land that can heal as nothing else, if you'll let it."

Turning from him, Merrill walked away. He was wise beyond his years, this man with the face of a not so faultless archangel, and the strength and manner of a gruff, but kindhearted bear. There was serenity here, the tranquility of a million years. The peace she needed to fill the dark void of her soul.

Tynan O'Hara watched and waited, sensing her conflict, tamping down the urge to take her in his arms and comfort her in her unnamed grief. Instead, wisely, he stood as he was, his hand curved at Shadow's muzzle.

"Will you stay?" he asked in a voice that barely rippled the aloof reserve she wore like a shield. "At least for a while."

Merrill turned to him. The shadows had not vanished, nor were the lines any less distressing, but there was a subtle ease in her manner.

A freshening breeze stirred where there had been none and in it lay a chill, a harbinger of the first snow. Catching back her hair, taming riotous curls in a natural and absent gesture, she nodded only once. As the wind nipped at her with baby teeth, she knew there was no going back. She had given her word, and her word was all she had left of the woman she'd been.

"I'll stay."

The wind whispered and muttered, and scratched softly at the eaves like a furtive banshee seeking crack or crevice to slip through. A warm, sunny morning had become an overcast afternoon, and in the evening hours the temperature plummeted. As the season's first sprinkle of snow began its patter against roof and windows, the night was fathomless black and frigid. But the house was warm and comfortable, and filled with soft light. A bulwark of security and tranquility in the midst of the storm.

In the great room, a fire crackled and danced in a fireplace that was one of three on the ground floor that shared the same fieldstone chimney. One for each room of the tightly and ingeniously constructed building.

Overlooking the great room lay the gallery. Expansive, rich with dark polished wood, opening to a sweep of towering windows spanning both floors. A combination of sleeping loft, study, and workroom, if one included the small enclosure Ty considered his lair. Into which he disappeared often during the day, and always each evening. Leaving her to her own counsel and her own devices for long periods of time.

Merrill had been his guest at Land's End for more than a week and, as he'd promised, there was no interminable togetherness, no forced companionship. In fact, none at all unless she sought it. On the rare occasions she had, he proved himself a genial host, a learned and thought provoking conversationalist. Like most men of few words, he had the gift of making those few say much.

On this night, as on most, she'd chosen to be alone. Not in her room with its own cozy fire, but the great room, with the sprawl of windows bringing the magnificence of the night and the storm to her, yet sealing her away from it, keeping her safe. As red cedars tapped against their panes, and elongated squares of light fell from her reading lamp onto a dusting of snow, Merrill didn't question her reasons for choosing this room over her own. She simply stared into the fire, listened to the whispers of the coming of winter, and let her mind go blessedly blank.

From the gallery, where he'd begun spending most of his evenings, leaning quietly against the handrail Ty watched her. As she sat in a small circle of light, feet tucked by her on the leather sofa, one finger marking a place in the book she never read, he wondered what solace she sought in the fire.

Were there demons there, dancing in an inferno? Or had she

begun to find soothing magic in the ever changing flame as he did? Was this the first of common grounds? Could there be more?

Would she discover the same beauty, the same mesmerizing enchantment he found in the ebb and flow of the sky? Would she learn to read the billowing clouds hovering over mountains and valleys, and predict their message? On rainy days, would she hear the haunting music in the call of a crow echoing through the mist? Or, as he, with each first snowfall on a quiet night, would she feel a sense of waiting in the utter stillness of the land? Would she welcome the underlying peace deepening and growing beneath the lacy pattern of each windblown flake?

Would she know, then, why he found this place riveting and captivating? And understand that he felt Montana had chosen him by answering his needs above all, as no other place in the world?

Ty wondered, and he questioned. Eight days and he hadn't a clue to what she felt, or thought, or wanted. Eight days and she was as much a paradox as from the first. As mysterious, as fascinating, intruding on his thoughts, but never the routine of his life.

She was such a silent little thing, there were times he almost convinced himself he could put her from his mind. Then, with the soft drift of her perfume and the silky rustle of her clothing, or a rare, quiet sigh and the pad of an even quieter footstep, she was there—in his thoughts. Consuming, captivating, drawing him ever deeper into the spell of her allure.

It wasn't that she crept or scuttled about avoiding him. She was simply subdued and unobtrusive. He wondered how much of her behavior was inherent, how much was her training, how much the product of the grief that tarnished her world.

"Who are you really, Merrill Santiago? What are you? What about you intrigues me?" he mused in an undertone she could not hear. For days, as he'd gone about his chores and obligations, he'd found himself asking these same questions. With never any explanation.

Nor had he any explanation for his own behavior. Why had he reversed himself so quickly and so completely? What had she touched in him that he would want so much to help her? And why did he so often find himself watching her, as he did now, puzzling about her, seeking the key to unraveling the mystery?

A log on the fire shifted, sending a shower of sparks over the hearth, and for a moment the fire burned brighter. In the radiance of the spitting roar of flames, she seemed smaller and so fragile he wanted to wrap himself around her, to hold her and guard her, fending off her demons.

Shadow must have felt as concerned as his master, Ty concluded, for as the furor of the fire calmed, the wolf rose from his place by the hearth and padded to her. Laying his great head on her knee, his eyes turned to her face, he waited for her caress.

"Well, hello," she said with a tremor of surprise. "Feeling lonely, are you?"

The timbre of her voice was low, a pleasing contralto. Her words, usually almost lifeless, were gently teasing as she stroked the huge head tentatively at first, and then with delight. "Ahh, you like that, do you?"

Shadow shivered, as excited as a puppy. His tail bludgeoned the edge of the sofa as he nudged at her hand begging that she continue.

"You want more, huh?" Her fingers raked through the heavy, dark coat, and scratched at his ears and nose. Her short trill of laughter sent another shiver of puppylike delight rushing through this creature who looked as if he should be ranging the hills, leading his pack. "Some great, terrible brute you are. Better mind your p's and q's or someone will find out your secret. Then all the world will know you're a teddy bear, not a devil dog."

Shadow rumbled a shameless agreement, and closed his eyes as he gave himself up to her loving touch.

As easily and simply as that, Ty realized Shadow had done what he could not. Not yet. It was far too soon for any but the most careful overture. She was too withdrawn to allow more than the slightest human trespass of the walls with which she guarded her thoughts and herself.

But Shadow hadn't cared about walls or trespass. As was his way with all hurt and wounded humans, he'd bided his time, waited for a dreamy, tranquil moment, then he'd simply stormed her bastion and wriggled his way into her heart.

From his separate and lofty vantage, Ty listened as she murmured teasing, loving words of sense and nonsense to a wild beast that was tame only because he chose to be, outweighed her by half again, and could snap the fingers that stroked his muzzle with a single clench of razor-sharp teeth. And when she dropped her book to wrap her arms around the massive neck and bury her face in the gleaming midnight fur, he smiled.

"Good boy," he murmured only to himself. With Shadow's help, this small, tormented woman with the heart and mane of a lioness had taken one minute step toward healing. But there was more to come, and it would be more difficult. More pain filled.

The wind whispered and muttered, and scratched at the eaves. The night was fathomless and frigid. The snow fell.

A fire smoldered and began to burn low beyond a hearth of stone. And a great wolf worked his magic. Little changed, but in a heartbeat, nothing was the same.

"It's time, Val," a brother said to his sister who was twenty-five hundred miles away. As far south as he was north. "Time to begin what you intended when you sent your bruised and grieving friend to the mountain wilderness. When you sent her to me."

The wind whispered, the fire smoldered, the snow continued to fall. And Tynan O'Hara descended from his lair.

Two

The muffled tap of his boot heels on the winding staircase was lost in the lowing of the wind. For a man who topped six feet two, and carried most of his weight in the brawn of chest and arms, he moved with startling ease. Narrow hips and waist and lean, hard muscled thighs bespoke more the physique of a born horseman and a working cowboy than one so comfortable afoot.

He reached the landing slowly, his light, unhurried step once more belying his size. His stride, when he crossed the room to the fireplace, was long and sure with fluid grace. Handsome, masculine grace, as quiet as a peaceful dream. Beneath the sheltering ruffle of lowered lashes, with her cheek resting against Shadow's furry neck, Merrill watched with somnolent, unseeing eyes as he knelt to the dying fire.

As if only waiting his attendance another log burned through, tumbling into ash. A burst of blue tipped flame leapt and danced in a weaving column. Embers shattering into tiny sparks scattered in a spangled shower of shooting stars.

The minor chaos of this scintillating display drew her from the drifting, pain numbing retreat of her mind. Wrenching away from Shadow, she turned her bewildered, unfocused regard to Ty, the fire, then Ty again.

For a surreal instant this was part of a dream. This striking figure who moved more quietly than the wind was an illusion. Not flesh and blood. Not real.

"Forgive me." The apology spilled through the careful guard of a tender heart as he absorbed the lost look on her face. "I shouldn't have disturbed you."

Dismayed, she drew a long, hard breath. Exhaling slowly, walking a precarious tightrope between past and present, skirting memories hovering forever at the edge of her mind, she oriented herself. This was Montana. The tap at the window was wind driven snow. The dusky, featureless image etched by the fire at his back was Tynan O'Hara and inescapably real.

This is Montana, she began the litany again. Montana, not... *Stop!*

She didn't want to think of that, wouldn't think of it. Recovering from a near misstep, she managed a calm assurance. "There's nothing to forgive, you didn't disturb me."

"You were deep in thought."

"Not really." She shook her head, not willing to explain she had retreated to a place in her mind, a small lightless void where she didn't have to think. "I was just..." She could offer neither a logical explanation, nor a good lie. A curt jerk of her head dismissed the effort. "You didn't disturb me."

"Just enjoying Shadow's company?" he supplied for her and, to give her time to recover, busied himself with the wood box.

Realizing her fingers had stolen again into the dark rich pelt of the wolf-dog, she took her hand away. Clasping one over the other in joined fists, she rested them on her knee. "I shouldn't, I suppose."

Halting in midmotion, a log balanced in his palm, he turned from his chore. For an instant, glinting firelight marked the look of mild surprise on the chiseled planes of his face. In another, whatever his expression might reveal was shrouded again in darkness. "Why on earth should you not?"

Her fingers flexed, tightening over the backs of her hands. "Some people would resent the interference. Consider it the corrupting of a watchdog."

"Corrupting?" he laughed softly. "In the first place it couldn't be done. Shadow's too much a free thinker for that, far too much his own person. In the second, I'm not some people, Merrill, and Shadow isn't my watchdog. He isn't my anything. He belongs to himself, not to me."

At her look of askance he laid the log aside, and hunkered down on the floor. With one arm braced on his knee, he leaned against the stone ledge of the hearth. "Shadow's been with me a number of years, but I didn't choose him. He chose me."

Doubting as he intended she should, she commented skeptically, "In the middle of nowhere, a wolf, where wolves rarely exist, chooses you?"

"Three-quarters wolf, and a bit more," Ty said, though he knew the teasing reminder was quite unnecessary. "Enough to be mistaken as pure wolf."

"So you said." It was never the wolf part Merrill questioned. No one would question that, only the ratio.

"So my sister the vet estimates."

Searching for a name, Merrill walked the tightrope again. Selective memory served. "Patience."

"Val has told you about her?" A small shift of his foot, a slight twist of his body and his face turned in profile. The flickering blaze again marked the stalwart features and cast a sheen of silver and gold over the blackness of his hair.

"Only that she's the youngest, and a veterinarian." Merrill saw a strong likeness to Valentina in him. His hair a little darker. His eyes, she remembered, were a little paler blue, yet the same. The arching brows were thicker, the chin as noble, as stubborn. She wondered if his mouth beneath the dark slash of his mustache was as generous in its masculinity.

Now that she let herself see it, the resemblance was uncanny. But Valentina was part of The Black Watch, and however strong their new friendship, she didn't want to think of anyone or anything to do with the clandestine organization. Even Patience, the younger O'Hara, was indirectly connected. Not by profession, but by marriage and one of those unexpected coincidences proving one must always expect the unexpected. Matthew Winter Sky, half French, half Apache, the mythical and mystical tracker of The Watch, had survived a rattlesnake bite and was alive and well because of the love and care of Patience O'Hara.

Merrill shook the recollection aside. Tonight the path of all thoughts seemed determined to lead to forbidden territory. If she must think at all, she wanted it to be of snowy nights and Shadow.

"So," she began, turning the conversation back on track. "This great, hulking sweetheart chose you."

"You could say that."

"How?"

"Long story."

"We have the night, don't we?" She cast a look at the window where snow had begun to accumulate in miniature drifts over the sill. "You aren't expecting anyone in this blizzard, are you?"

Ty would have laughed at calling this first, early dusting a blizzard, but he saw she was utterly serious. "We have the night," he agreed, careful to do nothing to spoil this tenuous, first thread of communication. "And no one is slated to come calling."

Shadow had sat on his haunches at her feet, his piercing blue gaze turning from his human companions to the window and back again. Ty knew that a part of the animal wanted to be away, answering the call of his blood, running wild and free, prancing and tumbling and licking at the flying flakes like a puppy. It was always the same with the first snow.

If he'd asked, Ty would have opened the door and let him go. But he didn't ask. He'd elected instead, to stay by Merrill.

With one last look at the window, and one for Ty, Shadow sighed and laid his head in her lap.

There would be other snows.

Merrill didn't smile. It was too soon for that. But a look of delight eased the sadness in her face. And as she bent to the wolf, her gold streaked curls mingling with the ebony pelt, Ty waited and watched.

She was a little thing. He couldn't get past that. It was always his second thought when he thought of her, his second impression with each rare encounter. The first, each time, was of dark, grieving sadness. Sadness where there should be laughter and light.

It was that and the unexpectedness of her that touched his heart. A warrior's heart, with a tender streak no better hidden than her sorrow. When he'd first seen her, standing fragile and vulnerable and golden in the sun, he'd known he wouldn't turn her away from his winter sanctum. Promises to Val aside, he couldn't turn her away.

So he watched them in his home, the wolf who was of the night, the woman who should have been sunlight. He watched her and learned.

A man should smile when he watched a beautiful woman. But he didn't.

For eight days, a week of days and one more, she'd shared his home, and he knew her little better than on the first. In those days they'd co-existed, spending little time in the same room, exchanging fewer words. After seeing to her needs and her comfort on that first encounter, keeping to his own schedule, he'd given her a wide berth, letting her settle in as she would. Rising at dawn each morning, after a quick and solitary breakfast, he cleared out, giving her space and time to work through her troubles. Throwing himself with unnecessary vigor into the necessary check of fences and animals, he tried not to think of her. Tried not to worry.

Lunch was early. A quick sandwich or biscuits and beans on whichever part of the spread he was working. When his day brought him back to the central part of the ranch and the house, there was never evidence that she'd left her room or eaten at all.

Following an established pattern, the first of the afternoon he devoted to exercising the horses he'd kept for the winter. Midafternoon was devoted to private and professional concerns. The last he spent in preparing dinner. The one meal for which he insisted she join him, after two days of discovering she forgot to eat without the reminder.

As with most ranchers who remained bachelors into maturity in this isolated country, he was a passable cook. Actually, better than passable. Not a gourmet, he would be first to admit, but definitely better than passable.

He could set an enticing table too. Nothing elaborate, just pleasant. When she hadn't resisted his stipulation that they share the evening meal, to encourage her appetite and give her pleasure, he put away the battered tin he used when the summer guests were gone, and brought out unique settings of hauntingly beautiful Native American design. An odd and striking mix with the delicate Irish linen he brought from storage, and with the crystal he always favored for his wines. Odd, striking, but one that worked.

She'd sat at his table. She'd eaten meager portions of the food he put before her agreeably, but silently. And when the meal was finished, her offers to clean the kitchen kindly and firmly refused, she returned as silently to her room. With the last dish put away, and coffee readied for the morning, Ty retired as tacitly to his lair and his computer.

A routine that seemed carved in stone. Then, to his pleased wonder, she began to venture into the great room. At first, just to sit, empty-handed, empty-eyed, uninterested. Certainly not in search of company. More as if with familiarity the walls of her room had become confining, driving her to seek out a change of territory. Next came the restless wandering, an incurious pacing. Then discreet and well-mannered exploration, the quickening of an intellect that wouldn't be denied.

And thus, another pattern evolved. Sometimes she read. Sometimes not. Sometimes she only sat, her mind far removed from this little part of her world. But it was another step toward healing.

From his desk he heard her each night, rifling through books, sighing softly and unaware, as she sat before the fire. She had taken each small step forward, yet remained as silent and withdrawn as if she were still secreted in her room. Now Shadow, with his uncanny instincts, had drawn her out. And if it was of Shadow she wished to hear, she would.

First he attended the fire, stacking logs on smoldering coals until it blazed with renewed vigor. Driven away from the hearth by the heat, he crossed to a cabinet, poured a pale cognac into two short-stemmed glasses. Palming them, he celebrated and enjoyed, again, the extraordinary communing and the deepening bond between woman and beast.

Her hair was a tumble of captured sunlight in the glow of firelight. Her body was delicate, too slender. And when she lifted her face from the wolf, she moved with the slightest easing of strain.

It was a little. It was enough, for now. It was a beginning.

Returning to her, Ty stood by her seat, anticipating the moment her amber gaze would lift to his. Her head tilted as he had come to expect, her look was solemn and steady. He saw the strength there, and the courage. Merrill Santiago wasn't lost, only battered and bruised.

With care, bruises healed. In time.

As she took the glass from him, her fingertips brushed his, a singularly pleasant sensation accompanied by a murmur of thanks. He felt that somber study on his body and the memory of her fingers tingling his as he settled down and deep into the cushions of the sofa across from her.

"You were going to tell me about Shadow, and how he came to be your...shall I say...partner and friend?" Her words were measured and unhurried, her voice husky. The gaze as steady.

"I was, wasn't I? My partner and friend...you make an apt assessment, one few others grasp." He stared into the fire and listened to the storm. Judging the weakening of its force, content that tomorrow promised to be a rare and pristine day, he launched into his story.

"I'd been here only a few months, and the cabin and barns were hardly completed before winter struck. An early one. Earlier than this. On its heels a pack of wolves and wild dogs ranged over the border from Canada. They were here, there. Everywhere and nowhere. For weeks they played havoc with the cattle on ranches for miles around. Moving like phantoms, they were always a step ahead of the range hands. Sometimes a step behind, on their back trail.

"If a herd was due to be shifted to safer ground, they were there first." Cognac swirled in the glass as he flexed and turned his wrist. "The Indians called them Ghost Wolves, saying they moved through the valleys and over the mountains, leaving no tracks, no sign, like shadows on a dark day."

"Shadows," Merrill murmured and looked down at their namesake.

"Wolves," he mused, "out of nowhere. Wolves where there had been none for so long. Phantom and phenomenon. Naturally the rangers and environmentalists and all the bureaucrats imaginable were called in by the authorities. But some of the smaller stockmen were facing disaster and were far too worried and too antsy to wait for their proposed remedies to work. Taking matters into their own hands, they brought in people of their own.

"Bounty hunters." His face was wooden, but there was contempt in his tone. "These killers who called themselves professionals hunted and slaughtered at will. Trapping, shooting and butchering, even poisoning anything on four feet that wasn't a cow or a horse."

A grim smile tugged at his mustache. "Even goats and sheep, and sometimes farm dogs were at risk when they were at their baiting and trigger-happy worst.

"During most of the furor, I was spared the wolves and the hunters. Then, one day I found one of them in the woods. A magnificent wolf, the biggest female I'd ever seen, and as black as night." The glass moved, cognac swirled. "She'd been shot. I don't know when or where, or how far she'd run before she bled out. She had pups and three of the litter were with her. When I blundered onto her body, they ran away, scattering into the woods.

"After I buried her I searched for them." The ripple of his shoulders, as he brought the glass to his lips, called attention to their power. "No luck."

"Yet Shadow's here." As she said his name again, the great creature made a pleading sound deep in his throat and nudged his nose at her knee. Both her hands were clenched around her glass. Now she eased one away to stroke the wolf, her fingers gliding comfortably now down his muzzle in the familiar caress he sought.

Ty savored the pretty picture they made, how natural it seemed in his home. He realized that, with the easy unclenching of her hands and the caress of the wolf, the fissure in the bastion that defended her heart had become a crack.

Settling deeper into the cushions of the sofa, he propped an ankle on his knee. "There were signs of the pack around for days," he continued, picking up the thread of his narrative. "I'd never seen such tracks. Monstrous, but light, as if the Indians were right."

"Ghost Wolves."

"I lost a colt." He turned pensive with the telling of it, then shrugged away the loss. "He was the last. As mysteriously as they came, the wolves were gone."

Taking her empty glass from her, he returned it to the bar. His half smile was rueful. "As I said, long story."

"Not so long." Beyond her response to the wolf, Merrill had hardly moved throughout the revelation, as fascinated with his voice, his choice of words, his manner of speaking as with the story. Ghost Wolves, moving like Shadows, phantoms— he had a way with words, a nice touch. "You weave a remarkable story, but it isn't finished."

"Not yet." Ty swung about, by habit gauging the drift of snow accumulating in the corners of windowpanes. He was quiet for the space of a heartbeat, remembering the tiny ball of fur stumbling and tumbling after him on legs too short and feet too large. A pup attached to a boot heel as firmly as the name he'd been given.

Fate? Providence? One creature sensing the need of another? More than coincidence, or only that? Ty would never know.

It didn't matter.

All that mattered was that the tiny pup that became the great wolf, had come to him. When he turned again, Ty's lips softened into a fond smile. "Five days later, when the bounty hunters were gone, as if he knew by instinct he was safe, a pup walked out of the woods. He never left."

"Shadow, choosing you."

"After a fashion. His fashion."

"Safe," she mused. "Yet Valentina says you're a hunter."

He hesitated so long she thought he wouldn't answer. Taking his glass from the table, he drained a final, clinging drop from it. His blue gaze pierced her like a shard of ice. "I was. Once. But not for bounty." Setting the glass down on the bar with exaggerated care, he said with a calm that sent shivers down a wary spine, "Never for bounty."

Merrill held his fierce stare. There was darkness in his eyes. More than anger, more than loathing. Had she hit a nerve? Was there more reason for *Fini Terre* than a man seeking his livelihood in a land as beautiful as paradise?

Valentina called it his Journey's End.

Journey from where? From what?

"My turn to apologize," she managed, and was surprised to find she meant it.

"There's no need to apologize for the truth."

"You make it sound as if you were more than a casual hunter?"

"I have been. I was. A long time ago." He moved away from the bar, returning to the hearth. Subject closed.

His broad back brooked no questions as he banked smoldering coals and readied the fire for the night. Rising from the completed task, he turned again to her. The hard edges had

eased from his face, the darkness from his eyes. "It's late."
His gaze flicked to the book she'd laid aside, lingered, then
slid away. "I'll leave you to your reading."

As silently as he'd come, he left her.

Listening as the tap of his step faded from the stairs, she
glanced down at the book. A mystery with a provocative
theme that on a glance promised to pass the time that lay
heavy on heart and mind. A temporary escape within the reach
of her fingertips, but she didn't pick it up.

Snow fell thinly now, clinging wetly to the window with
its soft patter. The fire leapt and weaved in twining columns.
Shadow sighed and lay at her feet.

Merrill thought only of the man who had given her sanctuary from the demons that plagued her. She thought and she
wondered. The spirited curiosity lying dulled and dormant for
weeks and months began to kindle.

Ty stopped short in the kitchen doorway, discovering Merrill Santiago was as lovely at dawn as any other hour.

When he'd first heard her stirring, a sixth sense that never
rested drawing him from a light sleep, he'd been alarmed. Was
she ill? Hurt? Had she decided she must leave?

That brought him lurching from his bed, reaching for clothing thrown over a chair the night before. His hands had been
clumsy with zippers and buttons in his urgency. A rare circumstance for Tynan O'Hara. Sucking in a long, harsh breath,
he'd forced himself to slow down, to calm down. To listen
and think, attuning again to the instinct that had awakened
him. Instincts that had always served him well.

The sounds he heard were politely guarded, not furtive. Little more than a rustle, a tiny disturbance of the air that would
have gone unnoticed except at an hour when the house was a
well of unbroken calm. The fragrance of brewing coffee had
drifted to the gallery and with another long breath he had
smiled. One who was hurt, or ill, or absconding wouldn't take
the time to make coffee.

He'd given her a half hour before coming down from his

lair. Letting her immerse herself in the solitude of the morning, the glory of first light on virgin snow. It was a time he found most peaceful. A time that brought peace to him. When he'd gone to her at last, he'd moved quietly down the stairs, hoping without shame for this moment.

Leaning a shoulder against the smooth planed arch of the door, he let himself be charmed by the glory of a golden woman captured in the golden reflections of sunrise. Yes, she was truly lovely and, for a rare moment, at peace.

Merrill sat before the kitchen windows marveling at the utter beauty of the beginning day. Her face, in profile, was dreamy, even serene. Coffee steamed from a cup on the table. Shadow sat by her side, a flick of his ears the only acknowledgment of Ty.

Dawn was brighter for the snow. The red-gold hues of the sky glinting over it painted the world in a fiery rainbow of color. The chill of night lingered, lightly frosting the windows. But with the advent of the sun the temperatures would rise, and the day promised to be pleasing. Later there might be snow so deep he would have to dig through it to clear a path from the house to the barns and storage buildings. But for now, for today, this small part of Montana was a fairyland dusted with glittering, sun spangled white.

Merrill couldn't have chosen better for the next step of her return to the world. Nor, in his judgment, a better world.

"Good morning." He kept his voice quiet. As quiet as his step as he joined her by the window.

"Mr. O'Hara." Surprise showed only in her eyes as she tilted her head toward him. "I didn't hear you come in."

"No problem." Dragging a chair from the table, he spun it around and sat across it as if it were a saddle. Folding his arms over the back, he grinned at her. "It's an easy thing to lose oneself in a Montana morning. Though there is a problem."

"I'm sorry," Merrill rushed in. "I saw the coffee was ready and I didn't think you'd mind." She started to rise. "I can make a fresh pot, if you like."

"No, Miss Santiago." He stopped her with a hand on her

forearm. "I don't mind and I don't need a fresh pot." He grinned again. "You can't corrupt my kitchen or my coffee any more than you can Shadow. You're welcome to anything, anytime. So sit."

"I could pour you a cup, at least." She sat on the edge of her chair, waiting to jump up the minute he released her.

"Sit. Stay," he said firmly as he swung out of his seat. "I can do that as well. I wouldn't know how to behave with someone serving me."

Merrill waited until he returned to the table before she spoke her concern. "You said there was a problem."

"There is." His sobering gaze met hers over the rim of his cup. He drank deeply, savoring the first cup of the day. The best cup of the day. Setting it aside, he refolded his hands over the chair. "A most serious problem."

"If you've changed your mind... If you'd like for me to leave..." Her hands curled tensely on the table. "I know I haven't been a model guest. It can't have been comfortable for you to have a strange woman intruding on your solitude." A week ago she would have been eager to go. Now she realized to her own amazement that she wanted to stay. For a while longer.

"Hey." Stroking a finger along the line of her jaw, Ty turned her face to his. A frisson of emotion he didn't stop to identify fluttered in his chest as he saw her disappointment. "I haven't changed my mind. I haven't been uncomfortable. And I don't want you to leave."

"But I've been..."

"You've been fine. Healing as you came here to do, in your own way. In your own time, Miss Santiago. *Miss Santiago.*" With the repetition of the name he sighed heavily and moved his hand down her throat and away. "That's the problem."

She looked at him blankly, not understanding. But he had her complete attention.

"The formality," he explained gently. "This mister and miss stuff is going be a waste of effort and breath if we're to be housemates for the winter."

"You want me to call you Tynan?"

"If you like. Tynan is fine, but Ty would be better. It's what my family and friends call me, and I'd like to think that considering the time we'll be together, we'll be friends."

"A nickname," Merrill said thoughtfully. "I've never had a nickname."

"You're joking." The smile that had begun to curl again beneath his mustache faded when he read his mistake in her expression. "You aren't joking."

"There were never nicknames in our family. At least not the sort that were called to our faces, nor that one would want repeated."

"A formal family, I take it." With no show of the affection pet names often revealed? he wondered.

"Military and male, for nearly a century. An attitude, a way of life at home, as much as a profession." She could have added an almost brutal adhering to the military formality that spilled over to childhood friendships. Affecting them, keeping them distant and virtually impossible.

"Military and male?" He asked to encourage her to continue. Last night she'd listened. Today he hoped she would speak and grow comfortable with him, establishing stronger lines of communication.

"Very military. Very male. I was the first girl child born in a long line of male progeny. Before the fact, my birth was heralded as cause for great celebration. I was to be that special child, the son who would mark a century for the Santiagos at West Point. For the space of a bitter and disappointed week, no one knew what to do with me.

"A female! Females were hand picked and accepted into the family by marriage, never born to it." Merrill bowed her head as if imagining that shocking day. "Yet there I was, born and bred, a Santiago."

"A beautiful disaster," Ty observed, with pity for the unexpected child fervent in his heart.

"Beautiful? Maybe, as all babies are. Disaster? Beyond a doubt. Then, recovering from his shock, if never his bitter disappointment, my father took charge. He decided, that with some minor adjustments, the family would go on as before. Tradition would be upheld. From that moment, on the strength of that decision, I was groomed for the day I would fulfill his dream.''

"Another Santiago fed like fodder to the military." Ty very carefully kept his escalating distaste for a man he'd never met from his voice.

Her stare was distant, looking into the past. Softly, her words more than a breath, less than a whisper, Merrill said, "My father never forgave me for refusing to go to The Point."

"You chose Duke University and languages instead." This he knew from the little Valentina had told him when she'd called to make certain Merrill had arrived safely, and to wheedle herself back into his good graces. "I've been told you have an astonishing gift for languages."

"I suppose you could call it that, or simply an affinity that came with exposure. My father moved around quite a lot, from base to base and country to country. Because not even he could bully the all male boarding school Santiagos have attended from time immemorial to ease the regulations and accept me, I stayed and traveled with the family. And, yes, I discovered first that languages were fascinating, then that they came easily for me, almost instinctively."

Shadow sighed and lay down at Merrill's feet. Ty knew the wolf had been hoping for a romp in the snow before it disappeared. But he knew, as well, that now that the furry protector had taken Merrill to his untamed heart, the loyal creature wouldn't leave her side.

"Your mother was supportive?"

Her hands were folded now in her lap. She looked down at them. "As much as she could be. It was difficult for her because she shared my father's view as strongly."

"Ahh, yes," Ty drawled drolly. "Of course she would. Because she'd been one of the chosen, no doubt." A woman as suited to the military as her man. No doubt there either. Ty had crossed paths with such men and women, and such families before. He was as well traveled as Merrill, but there the similarity stopped. Though he had little difficulty imagining the discipline, the unreasonable expectations of a martial martinet, nothing could have been more disparate than his own sprawling, comfortable family. As far as nicknames went, he'd had more than he could remember, ranging from professor to jughead. And finally settling in adulthood to Ty. "I can see that you must have been a shock to your family."

"A shock and a disappointment," she repeated. "From the day of my birth, and now."

She said it lightly, too lightly. Ty saw through the nonchalance to the little girl who first and last had been a failure. Damn them! he raged in heated silence, and wanted to take her in his arms and comfort her—the little girl and the woman—for past and present hurts. Instead he caught a rippling curl and wrapped it briefly around his finger, then watched it drift back to her shoulder.

"And no one ever called you Merry?" he murmured in a voice that had suddenly grown husky.

"Nicknames, loving names, should fit. Merry wouldn't have suited me as a child," she said with unconscious gravity. "It wouldn't now."

Ty let his look wander over her. Her hair was a tumble of rivulets in scintillating hues. Her eyes reminded of the darkened sand of a storm swept beach. Just now, with her solemn gaze on him, in the light of dawn, he could think of any number of endearing names that would describe her.

"Hey." Sliding from the chair he wheeled it about and put it back in place. "Are you hungry?"

Taken by surprise at the sudden switch, Merrill thought for a moment and discovered that she was. "As a matter of fact, I am."

"Famished?" He waggled his hand, his thumb and little finger tilting up and down. "Or only moderately?"

This time her answer came promptly. "Moderately."

"Good. How about a ride, then breakfast by a stream?"

"Breakfast by a stream?" She glanced out the window as

if she might have missed something in the course of their conversation. "In case you haven't noticed, this is Montana and there's snow out there."

"For now," he agreed. "But it will be gone by the time we reach the stream." When her expression turned skeptical, he laughed and couldn't keep himself from touching her cheek with the back of his hand. "Trust me in this. I know Montana."

"Maybe you know Montana, but you don't know if I ride."

Ty gazed down at her through narrowed eyes. He would almost swear he saw the beginnings of laughter on her face. "Do you?"

"Not well enough for the rodeo, but enough to know the front of a horse from the rear. I can manage to stay in the saddle on a sedate ride."

"Sedate, and you manage, huh?" She was leading him down the garden path, he was sure of it. A subtle tease, hinting at a wealth of humor temporarily weighted down by her troubles. Another step. Another beginning. "We ship most of the horses to lower pastures once the season's over, but I think I can find you a mount that fits the bill.

"You brought boots, I hope." He gave his approval of the full, comfortable shirt she wore, as well as the jeans belted snugly at her waist. With a jacket, both would do nicely. The delicate footwear, some sort of house slippers he deduced, left much to be desired.

"I have something that will suffice," she returned casually.

"Terrific. I can have the supplies we need assembled and meet you in the barn in five minutes. Will you need more than that?"

"You're sure about this?" Merrill cast another doubtful glance at the window. "We aren't going to get lost in a blizzard and go snow blind, are we?"

"This is hardly a blizzard, as you'll see later in the winter. We aren't going to be lost. And I assure you, sweetheart, I won't let anything happen to your enchanting eyes." The endearment, one he'd imagined only moments before, had been a simple slip of the tongue. He wasn't a man who normally went about calling virtual strangers familiar names, but it had seemed natural to think of her in those terms. It still seemed natural. Though, if she was as modern and as progressive in her thinking as her skills, she would very probably have his bloody scalp hanging from her belt for the diminution.

Yeah, maybe he should apologize. Should, he thought with little remorse, but wouldn't.

Merrill was far less concerned with the slip than with her reaction to it. If this was a bar and he a stranger, he would be agonizing over his tenderest parts. But on a snowy morning at *Fini Terre,* and coming from Ty who looked at her through caring eyes, the casual endearment filled her with a warm, blushing glow.

Suddenly, it was wonderful to feel something more than the cold emptiness of guilt. And the wonder of it was there for Ty to see in the muted animation in her manner when she stepped away from the table. "Five minutes?" she considered. "That should be quite enough."

When she would have gone to her room, his hand closing over her shoulder detained her. Her face was flushed and luminous, her mouth soft and dewy. For a mad moment he wondered if she would taste as delicious as he imagined.

A gold tipped brow arched in question as she stood motionless beneath his hand.

"I suppose this means you've decided to trust me after all." His voice was hoarse from the sudden need to take her in his arms, to steal the kiss he wanted so badly.

Her smile was slow, and real, but with the ever present sadness lurking beneath it. She was conscious of the weight of his hand. The warmth, the strength, hers for the taking. For her to trust. For the winter.

"Yes, Ty," she murmured, lingering a heartbeat over his name as she lifted her gaze to his. "I suppose it does."

Three

He'd been snookered. Hoodwinked. Hustled and had.

Led down the garden path would be putting it mildly.

He knew it when he looked over the back of the horse he was saddling and found her watching him from the corral fence. Her jeans were the same, and the shirt. The jacket was of a matching denim. Not as faded, but enough that he knew it was a working jacket, not purely the decorative complement of a tenderfoot's idea of ranch wear.

Sensible, practical, but the real giveaway was her boots. Or rather not boots. She wore moccasins, wrapped and laced, and tied at the knee. The same footwear favored by some of the Indians who worked with him as guides and wranglers through the short tourist season. Not as an affectation, nor for show, but comfortable, practical footwear for the skilled and intuitive rider.

His arms folded across the saddle, his hat tilted back a notch, he studied her from the Stetson that was far from new, to moccasins that were at least as old. A wry smile crinkled in fanning lines about his eyes. A flip of his finger moved the hat brim back another notch. "Sedate, huh?"

Merrill only nodded. The sun was at her shoulder, its muted fire casting provocative shadows beneath her cheekbones and turning her skin luminous. She'd taken a minute to braid her hair. But a minute was never enough to completely tame her curling mane. Tendrils escaped and drifted like mists about her face.

Ty wondered what it would be like to paint, to be able to capture on canvas the time, the place, this woman, forever.

The horse, a small, pretty mare, stamped a hoof and flicked an ear signaling an eagerness to be away. "Ho, girl." Ty tapped her neck and stroked her, but kept his gaze on Merrill. A gaze that swept over her again, taking in every detail, the gear, the posture, the lithe, agile body. The mischief he couldn't see, but knew was lurking there. He hoped was lurking there.

"You know one end of a horse from another, do you?" he asked soberly, picking up the threads of the conversation they'd had in the kitchen as if it had never been interrupted.

"The tall end is the front." The reply was given just as soberly, without a ripple of change in her expression.

"And which side to mount from?" He continued the unnecessary catechism.

"Your side, if you're a cowboy."

"And if you're not a cowboy or a cowgirl?"

"My side." Merrill stayed by the fence. Her expression never altering.

"Indian fashion?"

"My first riding lesson was in Argentina." A comment that might have been apropos of nothing, a digression, per chance a convoluted diversion. But not when it came from Merrill.

As she paused, his head angled and a brow lofted as he tried to make the connection. "Argentina."

"I was seven."

She was setting him up for the punch line, that would be the explanation for her dress, the definitive explanation. If she needed a straight man, he would oblige her. Recalling the wonderfully sprawling pampas of that country, with its dashing and daring riders, and imagining a tiny seven-year-old among them, he prompted, "You were seven, your father was stationed there."

"My father was part of a sort of a roving diplomatic corps. I didn't understand his work then, I don't now. We'd been there a few weeks when he deemed it was time I learned to ride."

"A logical decision, given the nature of the country and the skill of its riders."

"Quite logical," Merrill agreed. "But my first instructor was..."

"A gaucho." Who better to teach her, Ty wondered, than one of Argentina's flamboyant versions of the cowboy?

"A Dakota." She chuckled under her breath as she corrected his logical assumption. "A Teton Sioux, and my father's aide for a long time. His rank was lieutenant, his military name was Matt Danvers, but I preferred his tribal name, Tall Bear."

"Tall Bear taught you to ride as he would."

"Not in the beginning."

"Not until he recognized the rapport." Ty's observation was based on more than supposition. He had seen it before. With his own riders as they took an interest in one of the guests who exhibited the unique quality that would make a superb rider. Sometimes it was one of the children. Sometimes an adult. But always there was something that set them apart. An undefinable element, more sensed than understood. Yet surely and simply there.

"Tall Bear began to teach me the Indian way when he realized we liked each other, the horses and I."

As did the child and the Sioux, Ty thought with certainty. What chance would even the heart of a warrior have with a golden child as she must have been? Chattering, no doubt, in record time, in his native dialect.

He had no more trouble imagining the sort of man her instructor had been, than he did the child. The Blackfeet and the Sioux were his neighbors, if one used the term loosely. Several men of each tribe worked for him in summer, leaving reservations situated on the east side of Glacier, the national park separating Montana into an entity with two personalities.

Throughout history the Sioux had become the paradigm of the fighting American Indian. The men who rode for him were living proof of it. Perhaps they weren't quite so warlike. Perhaps the fringed and beaded buckskins, and war bonnets of eagle feathers had been replaced by jeans and Stetsons, but the bloods were still tall and well proportioned. Their features still starkly dramatic with high-bridged noses and broad cheekbones.

Once they had been bold and arrogant warriors, splendid and contemptuous in their conviction of superiority. With this bold arrogance they had fought their Indian enemies for more than two hundred years. With the same zeal they fought the white invaders for fifty more.

In the beginning they had fought on foot. But was it little wonder that with the acquisition of the horse, they had become masterful horsemen? Mounted, they had, truly, been and were without peer. And always courageous to the extremes of foolhardy. Certainly they no longer warred among themselves, nor with the whites. But little else had changed. They were still bold, still arrogant, still as fearless and, sometimes, as foolhardy. And they remained horsemen without peer.

One who had been chosen to be taught the way of the Sioux by a Sioux, would be a rider, indeed.

Ty's gaze narrowed, fine lines crinkled at the corners of his eyes. Through lowered lashes he studied her with new perspective, seeing more than the small stature, the troubled fragility. There was strength here, tensile strength surpassing any dearth of physical size and uncertainty. The quality he'd glimpsed the night before. Spirit that needed only the time Valentina had asked him to give.

The curiosity that had drawn her from her room, then led

her to explore her new surroundings was the first of its res-
urrection. The mischief, this subdued chicanery a continuation.

In the mood of the game, for the hopeful pleasure of seeing
her smile and hearing her laugh, he said, "He taught you how
to mount, and not to fall off. So long as the ride is...." Hesitating he kept his gaze on her, waiting for her to fill in the
word.

"Sedate," she supplied on cue.

"Ahh, yes," Ty nodded. "That's it, sedate."

"The horse understands that, I hope."

"She understands." He stroked the mare's mane, smoothing
it over the bowed neck. "Tempest has been cooped up in the
barn and the corral for a few days now, I imagine she's up
for a ride. Any kind of ride."

"I suppose there's a story or a message behind the name."

"There is. One of the wranglers christened her that since
she's inclined to kick her heels up on early mornings. Particularly in the first snow." He petted and stroked the mare again.
"Loves the white stuff nearly as much as Shadow does. While
he leaps around and tumbles in it like a pup, she races and
slides and dances. Best cold weather horse I've ever seen."

"Tempest." Merrill repeated.

"As in a teapot."

She felt the laughter bubble in her chest. It had been so long
since she'd truly laughed she was almost giddy with it. Tynan
O'Hara made her smile. She hoped he always would.

Sensing the mood, Shadow barked and nipped at the fringe
of her moccasins. He was ready to play, or ready to run. The
mare chose that time to sidle away, bucking a little as if to
live up to the reputation she'd just been given.

"I think the animals are trying to tell us something." Ty
tipped his hat from his head, sweeping it to the prerequisite
position as he executed a gallant bow. Gallantry that came
natural to him, and seemed as right in the trampled snow of
a corral as any ballroom. His smile was as natural, as right,
as he asked, "Shall we ride, Miss Santiago?"

Merrill stepped between the rails, approached the horse, and paused before it. Her fingers trailed down the long bones from bang to soft muzzle. Her palm curled under the nibbling lips, letting the mare grow accustomed to the scent and taste of her. Then moving past the massive head, with her fingers curled now in the gleaming mane, she muttered in a low voice, "Delighted, Mr. O'Hara."

With the ease and skill that would have made Tall Bear burst with pride, she vaulted into the saddle.

Ty stepped closer, checking the cinch, adjusting the length of the stirrups she had ignored. When he was finished he moved back and found her frowning. "Something amiss?"

"I think I should tell you I've never ridden in snow," she admitted as she looked down at him. "Oddly enough, few of the countries we lived in had winters like this. If there were ever any that did," she shrugged, "my father always managed to be away for the season."

"A man of preferences," Ty growled in disgust, and couldn't say why this small aberration angered him even more. Perhaps it was simply that he'd chosen to be angry at the man in all things for past transgressions. It was, he realized, an exercise in futility. The battle had been fought. One he couldn't change. But, he decided, he didn't have to like the man who ruled the Santiagos with rigid tyranny.

No, he thought with satisfaction, he didn't have to like the man at all. Wheeling about, Ty whistled for his mount. The bay trotted from the barn, black mane flying, black stocking feet lifting high through the thin blanket of snow. Grasping the mane in one hand, in a flowing leap he lofted into the saddle as easily, as skillfully, as Merrill had done. Booted feet securely in stirrups, the Stetson returned to his head, the brim tugged low, he turned to her. "Tempest isn't sedate. In fact she wouldn't know the meaning of the word."

Merrill kept her face grave. "I suspected not."

"But she is surefooted. Snow is no more to her than ground wet from a shower. Trust her, let her decide where she can and cannot go. She won't let you down. She is truly the best cold weather horse on *Fini Terre*."

A small smile played at the edge of her mouth as Merrill wound the reins around her hand. "Thank you for that, at least."

"Still hungry."

She was! She truly was. "As a bear. A short bear."

Something flickered in her face, something unusual. A memory, first pleasant, then regretful. Ty almost missed it as the bay danced and reared, eager to be gone. As he settled the horse with a firm hand and a soft word, filing the incident away for a better time, he resolved to explore it, what provoked it, and to understand it. A better time than this.

Worried that the rare appetite would pass if delayed too long by this venture, keeping his voice casual and teasing, he asked, "Will an hour be too long?"

"In an hour I should be hungry as two bears."

She had recovered from her rueful recollection, but Ty didn't miss the small shift in her wording. Later, he promised himself, and eased his tight hold on the bay's reins. "Then let's ride, sweetheart. I don't have supplies enough for three bears."

"Let's." Merrill kicked Tempest with her moccasin clad heels, but the mare needed no more urging than the light prod. The small horse was a lightning bolt as it eagerly answered the command it awaited. As Ty suggested, Merrill gave the handsome creature its head, letting it go as it would. Learning on the run the personality of her mount as she'd been taught by the Sioux.

They flew together over the corral fence. Merrill as firmly seated as if she were part of the saddle. The moccasins were fast in the stirrups, but Ty knew she would ride as well bareback with legs hugging the horse, softly shod feet curled against the belly. Direction and perception made by touch unhampered with leather trappings.

He allowed himself the time to admire her, as he'd found himself doing with increasing frequency. She rode almost as well as Valentina, who was the best he'd ever seen, male, female, hussar, cossack, gaucho or cowboy.

Even the best of the Sioux would be hard-pressed to outride Val. But Merrill Santiago would be a close challenge. With a grin on his face and a touch of his heels setting his pacing bay into a leaping gallop, Tynan O'Hara, no tenderfoot in the saddle himself, took up the gauntlet.

The morning warmed rapidly as he expected. By the time they walked the horses through a small rocky stream, their breath was no longer visible and snow lingered only in small stubborn patches at the shady base of shrubs and trees.

Beyond the crest of the Continental Divide, before the hinterlands of the Great Plains, the forests would give way to other terrain, barren and windscarred. But now the land was lushly timbered. Here, nurtured by the vagaries of a mildly diminished Pacific Maritime climate found in only rare places, lay a wonderland rife with variety. Within a sweep of the eye, one could find lodgepole or juniper, Douglas fir or grand fir, Engelmann spruce or larch. Clinging to the towering folds of the mountains there would be the stalwart white bark pine, while along the forest floor rose the magnificent western red cedar and, weaving through them and by them, the hushed and great cathedrals of giant hemlocks.

As horses and riders splashed across the icy stream, it was a wonderland, indeed, with droplets and rivulets of melted snow glinting in evergreen jewels among the drooping conifers. Drawing his mount to a halt on the sloping bank, Ty stepped from the saddle and crossed to Merrill.

Laying a palm on Tempest's withers, he stood at her side. Smiling up into the flushed face of his guest, he asked, ''Well?'' A half turn and a gesture swept the small clearing and the enclosing hemlocks. ''Was it worth the ride?''

Following the path his gesture invited, she shifted in the saddle. For a time she seemed lost in her study, her look ranging high and low, tarrying here, returning there. ''Was it worth it?'' she repeated at last. Inhaling deeply, savoring the sweetness of air so pure it seemed to cleanse her, she returned her gaze to Ty and found him waiting patiently. ''This is truly beautiful. More than I dreamed it would be, and more than worth the ride.''

Ty waggled two fingers at her. "Two bears?"

"Definitely two." She looked again at the small meadow and the surrounding fortress of hemlocks. Sights and scents that spurred the senses and the appetite, as well. "Maybe two and a half."

"Then we'd better do something about getting some nourishment into you while I still have enough supplies to suffice." Before she could make any move to dismount, he reached for her, his hands clasping her waist, lifting her from the saddle.

"Ty!" She braced a hand on his shoulder as he swung her down. When her feet were firmly on the ground, she didn't take her hand away. Nor did he. She was oddly breathless and her voice roughened with it. "I'm perfectly capable of getting off a horse."

"Thanks to Tall Bear?"

"Exactly. I didn't need your help."

"I knew that," Ty answered mildly, aware that her hand slipped from his shoulder to his chest, her palm light and warm over his heart.

"Then why?"

In the distance, Shadow bayed, the domesticated part of him melding with the wild as he ran a small rodent to ground. The rush of sound grew faint, fading to a nuance, and then nothing. The meadow was tranquil again. The sun was warm. The stream danced and chuckled over stones left by leviathan spears of glacial ice thousands upon thousands of years before. An eagle streaked across an endless sky and plummeted from sight.

In a primitive land, a man fraught with primitive needs folded his hand over hers, keeping it hard against the thundering beat of his heart, and answered with the simple truth. "Why?" he parroted her question. "Because I wanted to.

"Now." He moved a step away, but did not release her. "We'd best see to that breakfast."

"Here?" Bewildered by his mood, not certain what she

should make of it, or that she should make anything of it at all, Merrill was grateful for the change in subjects. "Shall I gather wood?"

Her doubtful glance was already ranging over the clearing in search of fallen limbs dry enough to burn, when Ty laughed and drew her with him down a meandering path. "You don't think I brought you all this way to serve your first real appetite with food smoked by wet wood, do you?"

When she would have asked what else he could intend, considering that he'd packed in no dry tinder, the undergrowth thinned revealing a small shack. Ancient and dilapidated, its splintered wood blackened by age, the old homestead of some long-ago settler seemed to hunker into the land beneath the partial shelter of a mountain ash as aged.

The steps were tilted when they climbed them, the porch lurched and sagged when they crossed it. Yet both were solid underfoot. The door was secured by a small block of wood that spun on the single nail that held it in place. Leather strips served as hinges, swinging silently, neither creaking nor groaning as Ty pushed it open.

The homestead was comprised of a single room, with a tiny sleeping loft tucked overhead. Its floors were smoothly sanded, while the walls were rough sawn boards. In the only departure from the carefully preserved character, heavy slatted shutters stretched from ceiling to floor and corner to corner. A narrow table that could have been taken directly from a turn of the century Shaker household, stood before it. Banks of cabinets appearing as old marched along the opposite wall, while the back was dominated by a fireplace. A massive fireplace of chinked river stone that should have overwhelmed the small house, but did not. An old, iron stove, rivaling the one in his kitchen, ruled one corner, while wood boxes at each side of the hearth were filled and neatly stacked.

"Ahh," Merrill said as she moved to the fireplace and the heavy andirons that held a parcel of firewood needing only a match. "You've done this before, and keep it ready for the next time."

Ty drew a match from his pocket, scraped a thumbnail over it, and tossed it in a fiery arc into the maw of the fireplace. Dry wood literally exploded into flames, sending smoke swirling up the chimney in a rush before he answered.

"I stop by for a meal now and then, when time and circumstance coincide." Taking a metal rod from a hanger embedded in the rounded river stone, he rearranged a shifting log. "It's a pleasant spot, I enjoy it when I can, and keep a few supplies for the hopeful occasion."

"This doesn't serve as a line shack and it isn't part of the summer package? You don't bring the guests here for an outing?"

"No." He set the rod aside and leaned an elbow on the stripped tree trunk that served as a mantel. "Parts of *Fini Terre* are off limits. The house, the corrals closest to it, and this shack."

Having lived the congregate military life, Merrill understood the need to keep something private and for oneself. She didn't consider it selfish or self-centered, but simply a quiet pleasure, or dire necessity. With Tynan O'Hara, she was positive it was a case of quiet pleasure.

For his sister's sake he'd given her sanctuary and shared his home with a brooding stranger. Now he'd shared this, given her this. A shack on a lonely, isolated stream, but plainly more than a piece of history to him. She wondered why he'd brought her here?

While she pondered, Ty moved from the fire to the shuttered doors folding them back, revealing another group of doors. His task done, he faced her, and with his gallant bow presented a view to rival any on earth. Beyond him, beyond this wall of heavy beveled glass opened a sprawling deck, patio, terrace, Merrill had no idea what it should be called. Beyond that lay a startling panoramic view of a rolling meadow and the stream he'd promised, with hemlock touching the sky in stately spires. A pastoral magnificence to rival any she'd ever seen, any on earth.

"It's...." she shook her head, she hadn't the words for this, a gift to sooth the most troubled soul. "I can understand why you stop here when you can."

"The terrace catches the morning sun." He grinned. "The midday sun, and the evening sun. With your jacket, you should be warm enough to sit there while I build a fire in old Bessie." A flick of his wrist introduced the ancient stove. "While she's heating up, I'll see to the horses, then breakfast."

Drawing herself from a trancelike state, she insisted, "I can help."

"No." Ty clasped her arms, his hands sliding to the sloping curve of shoulder and nape, splayed fingers carefully kneading the painfully taut muscles they encountered. "You can help best by watching the fire, and the view."

Merrill knew not to argue, something in his manner warned it would be futile. She simply nodded again, and closing her eyes, gave herself to the bliss of the magic his fingers made.

His laugh was soft, the touch of his lips against her forehead softer, as he released her. "You look like a kitten that only needs the warm sunshine to make her purr. Go." He turned her from him, pushing her gently toward the terrace. "Sit. Listen to the stream, breathe air like none on earth. I'll be back before you know it."

The mouthwatering scent of frying bacon woke her. There was, she decided in her drowsy wisdom, no better complement for the marvelous perfume of an evergreen world. She hadn't meant to nap, when she found herself drifting had even struggled against it. But the cushion she'd found in a small closet off the side of the terrace, and the chaise were too comfortable and she'd fallen like a stone into her first truly restful sleep.

"Good morning...again," Ty said as he forked bacon from a smoking skillet. Coffee perked on another flat surface of the stove. The table was set, a pitcher of orange juice set on a shelf that served as sideboard.

Merrill stood in the doorway, yawning behind her hand. "Sorry, mountain air, nature's sleeping pill."

And pain, and turmoil, and sleep deprivation, Ty added to

a mental list. "I'm glad you did. Nothing could have given a better stamp of approval for this venture."

"You've been busy." Merrill watched him, moving competently, surely. As comfortable before the ancient stove as on a horse. When he broke eggs into the pan with a single hand, a feat she'd never mastered, and tossed the shells aside, he was utterly and completely and all the more masculine.

That he was handsome with his Stetson discarded and hanging on a peg, leaving his dark hair falling over his forehead didn't escape her either. More than handsome, an undeniable fact of which she was increasingly aware, one she couldn't risk dwelling on. Casting about for some distracting chore, she found nothing.

"Did you leave anything for me to do?" She strove to put a teasing plaintive note in the complaint.

"Sure," he retorted cheerfully. "The most important part."

"What would that be?" She asked, though she knew the answer.

"This." He guided her to a chair. Drawing it out, with the slightest pressure he seated her and returned to the stove to take a pan of biscuits from the warming closet at its top.

The terrace doors were thrown open, giving the effect of bringing the meadow and all it embraced to her. Rivaled by nothing, not even a painting.

Perhaps it was a vista to take her breath away, but the aroma of the foods he had prepared were more than any match for it. The appetite she thought sleep had stolen from her returned with ravenous might.

A plate appeared before her. Bacon, eggs. "Grits?" Leaning back in her chair, she looked up at him. "I haven't seen grits in years."

"My mom sends them. A distinctively Southern taste, I hope you like them." He was setting the biscuits and a jar of what was obviously homemade jam at her elbow. "And, before you ask, my culinary skill and patience don't extend to making jam. A neighbor dropped these by a few weeks ago."

"A neighbor," she drawled, remembering he had said the closest was forty miles away. "Just dropping by."

"Cora Franklin, just dropping by," he agreed and didn't explain that the forty was diminished considerably when cutting cross country. Rugged country that those who live in Montana had come to accept as part of everyday existence. "The jam was part of a care package her aunt sends regularly from Alabama. A very genteel, Southern lady, who considers Montana the jumping-off place. Or to translate, the end of the world. Wouldn't surprise me if Matilda thinks the Indians still go on the warpath, gathering the scalps of every white man who crosses their path."

"Matilda?"

"Matilda Prescott, ninety-two-year-old maiden lady, daughter of Jacob Prescott, founding father of Prescott, Alabama. She isn't quite clear on her history anymore, but she knows her way around a kitchen."

Ty worked as he spoke, setting a cup of steaming coffee before her, then uncorking a bottle of champagne. In a whisk of his wrist, the foaming brew was contained and poured along with the orange juice, into two stemmed balloon glasses.

"Mimosas in crystal? Here? Now?" Merrill blurted in surprise.

Cocking a wicked brow at her, Ty drawled, "You know a better place? A better time?"

Merrill considered, but only for the space of a glance at the land beyond the shack. "No better place on earth," she decided. "No better time."

"My sentiments, exactly. A celebration of your first time to really be a part of the country. And," he set the glass by chipped and mismatched crockery with a flourish befitting the finest table, "considering the hour, and that this is now more brunch than breakfast, it really isn't so sinful, is it?"

"Sinful?" Merrill lifted the mimosa from the table, savoring the feel of fine crystal as she drew another deep breath laden with the cleansing scents of Montana. Pleasures enhanced by the magic Ty had wrought. "The only thing that's sinful, is what a glutton I'm going to be."

Taking up his own glass, Ty touched it to hers. The bell-like ring of it seemed to fill the air. "I'll drink to that."

Glass in hand, Merrill strolled across the terrace. An addition obviously, but of wood as aged and rough as the shack itself. Ty had explained the material for it had come from a barn at the back. He was quite evidently as accomplished at demolition and construction as cooking.

"You did all of this?"

"Most of the work consisted of simple repair." Ty sat on the steps, watching as she glided back and forth. The sun was at its meridian, the snow only a memory, yet a definite harbinger of days to come. But for now the temperature was pleasant. The jacket she'd abandoned at breakfast still hung alongside his from a peg by the door. "All I did was use materials that were available."

"In keeping with the rest of the house," she observed. "Preserving its historic identity is important to you, isn't it? Everything about this place is important."

"It's a favorite, and what could be prettier than this?"

Merrill sat beside him on the step, her hand cradling her glass. "When you come here, it isn't always like this." She lifted the glass, letting the sun reflect in rainbows from it. As the shack should have been overwhelmed by the fireplace, the flawless crystal should have been a ridiculous mismatch and sorely out of place on the stark table with battered crockery. But it hadn't. It all seemed delightfully in keeping with her host and Montana.

A man and land of intriguing contrasts.

"When I come here, the fare is usually whatever is in my saddlebag. I don't bring in a packhorse, and I've never shared a mimosa on the terrace with a beautiful woman before."

Merrill blushed, something she thought she was long past. The pallor giving way to the wave of color, made her even more alluring in Ty's sight.

Tapping the rim of the glass, she listened again to the musical tone. Like the provisions, she knew these had been carefully wrapped and packed in for her pleasure. "Thank you for the compliment. For the day." A gesture encompassed the meadow, the stream, the stalwart hemlocks and the stark mountain rising against the horizon. "And thank you for this."

"My pleasure." Ty said no more, for a time they sat companionably in silence, listening to the stream, the rustle of the trees. He was first to speak. "If John Muir was right, if the ponderosa pine 'gives forth the finest music to the winds,' can the hemlock and red cedar be far behind?"

Merrill listened, there was music, in the trees, in the stream, in small breezes that played across the meadow. The day, itself, was music. "Tell me how this happened. How can there be snow, and then this?"

Ty hesitated, gathering his thoughts, then began. "Snow one day, moderate conditions the next. Confusing, to the say the least."

"The very least."

"It won't be when you stop to realize that when weather is concerned, Montana has a personality." At her look of askance, he smiled. "A split personality to be specific."

"Split personality."

"That's right."

"Which you are going to explain." She wasn't giving him the choice.

"Naturally."

He was silent again, gathering his thoughts. "It's simple really."

"It is?"

"All one needs to define Montana, is to understand it." As he had the wineglass the night before, with a flick of his wrist he turned the mimosa in his hand. "Most flatlanders and outsiders envision arctic weather when judging Montana. There are times it can be true. East of Glacier the winds do come out of the Arctic. Sometimes with as much force as a hundred miles an hour. Temperatures can vary in a twenty-four-hour period as much as a hundred degrees.

"*Fini Terre* is west of Glacier. The climate is milder, steadier, dominated by the weather patterns of the Pacific. There are winds. Yet little more than breezes when compared to the east. With the Pacific influence our weather changes by the day, the hour, the minute. Temperatures vary as rapidly, without the deadly extreme."

"Last night and today are examples of those extremes?" Merrill had listened raptly, hardly moving.

Ty set his glass aside and folded his hands over his knee. "Part and parcel. The time may come when we dig down to find the latch, but in relative terms, the conditions will be mild."

"Relative terms."

"It will be cold, Merrill. There will be snow. Predator and prey alike will migrate. The eagle will begin in October. Others later, some, like the mountain goat, not at all. But whatever winter brings, we will survive, I give you my word."

"With no more rides or days like this."

"Maybe, maybe not. The shack is never closed for winter."

"Why do you keep it as you have? And why private?" Merrill questioned abruptly, hardly aware that she'd asked, or needed specifics.

"Look around you, imagine children here. Can you think of a more perfect hideaway? When we were young, my brothers and sisters and I always had a place that was ours. Only ours."

Merrill looked around as he said, but could only imagine what it would be like to be a child, to have a place that was hers and hers alone. There had been no such luxury in her family. Her father had controlled everything and everyone. "You would like to have children?"

"Maybe. Someday."

"They would be fortunate."

Ty said nothing at first, remembering his own ebullient family. The fun, the daring adventure, the devotion. "I hope so, when or if my life comes to that."

Rousing from his reverie, he caught a flyaway curl between thumb and forefinger, tugging at it playfully, "If this is a game of twenty questions, I have one for you."

"One?" Merrill leaned away from him, aware that she missed the comforting brush of his arm against hers. "Only one?"

"For now."

"That means you reserve the right to ask more later."

"When the time comes."

Merrill was discovering his laconic replies could be maddening. "What time would that be?"

"Who knows?" Heavy shoulders shrugged beneath faded denim. Beyond the hillside, Shadow barked and yipped, closer now, his far ranging run finished. "We take each day as it comes, and learn what it allows."

"Today you would learn more about me." She kept her voice calm, her tone level. She owed him this, yet it frightened her to give anyone carte blanche. Even one as kind as Ty. "If there's something you need to know," her voice wobbled then, betraying her, "ask away."

He turned to her, gathering her hands in his. His blue gaze was piercing, his expression solemn. Too solemn. "I was wondering if you'd eaten too many biscuits and too much jam for the ride home." Then recalling the moment in the corral, the flicker of a memory, he made a logical guess, "Short Bear?"

For the blink of an eye and a sharply drawn breath his teasing question didn't register. Then the breath she'd caught and held flowed from her in a hearty laugh. "I'll manage." Then sobering, she admitted, "Until today, I'd forgotten the name Tall Bear gave me."

"Those were happy days?"

"The happiest."

Ty stood, keeping her in place with the weight of his hand

at her shoulder. "Then think of that, while I see to the fire and Bessie and close up the house."

"I can help."

"Next time."

He left her then, to think of happiest days.

And the next time.

Four

"**F**rom the looks of things, the weather's about to break." Merrill tugged at the fingers of her gloves, removing them one increment at a time. The pleasant warmth of the kitchen wrapped around her, taking away the chill of her morning ride. Though the autumn temperatures had remained steady and were still amazingly mild—by Montana standards she kept reminding herself—gloves were a necessity.

"The lady's a fast learner." Ty looked up from the sheaf of papers he was reading. "You've been here, what? Five weeks? Six? And you've learned to read weather signs."

"Learned to feel them is closer to the truth. It's cold, and the temperature is dropping fast."

Though she dismissed it, she had quickly acclimated. With the chameleon-like skills acquired in the vagabond life of a military brat, she'd taken on the protective coloration and manner the land required. Both figuratively and literally. On a glance, she would pass for a born-and-bred or long-settled Montanan.

Ty's gaze followed as she crossed the kitchen, bringing the cold fresh scent of a morning on the mountain range with her. A reminder that he'd been holed up in the house for days. "Consider these temperatures a blessing," he suggested tersely. "Doesn't happen often."

"So I've been told." Taking the pot of coffee that steamed eternally on the stove, she poured a cup. Waved the battered monstrosity toward Ty in an oblique invitation of a refill, then, at the declining shake of his head, returned it to the heated surface of the stove. "There were fewer eagles down by the river. Migration is beginning."

Ty made a noncommittal sound. She'd changed in more than manner and confidence since the first reclusive days of her stay with him. The pallid tones of her skin had warmed to a healthy flush. The flags of color drawn on her cheeks by the cold no longer looked like stark, mistaken slashes of rouge on a geisha's painted face. The thin hard edges of her body had softened into graceful curves as muscles had been honed and pounds regained.

The hurt and grief that had shadowed her dark eyes still lived deep inside her, would always be a part of her. But each day she coped. And each day it ruled her life a little less. If he'd found her beautiful in her sadness, now she was stunning. Unforgettable.

"Shadow found some tracks down by the lower meadow."

"What?" Ty's head snapped back.

"Shadow found some tracks down by the lower meadow and decided to investigate." She repeated and sipped from her cup, fighting down a shudder at the bitter taste she hadn't quite learned to enjoy despite the welcome heat. "I suppose he'll be along in a bit."

"What kind of tracks?" The ranch lay squarely in the winter range of mule deer and the whitetail. The bugling of bull elk was an integral part of the sounds of fall. The shyer, quieter moose occasionally wandered through. Any of these hooved creatures could be dangerous when cornered or crazed by pain or protective instinct. But the chance encounter would be uncommon. A grizzly was another matter. More calmly than he felt he asked, "Did you recognize them?"

"I wasn't close enough to see. All I can say is that he took off like a hound from hell on a hot trail." She sipped again, and this time the taste was not so shocking. "Whatever they were, must have been interesting."

"Must have." Shadow was seldom far from Merrill. Only something unusual could have drawn the wolf from her side. The gray wolf, perhaps the precursors and an explanation for Shadow's existence, had been naturally recolonizing in north-western Montana. Yet he was doubtful of wolves for there had been no recent indication a pack had ranged onto *Fini Terre.*

A grizzly would definitely be another matter. He'd seen signs of one in the spring. A big one judging from the mark-ings left on trees as it ripped apart the outer bark, skinning it back to feast on the sweeter, tenderer inner bark. A trail of the high, triangular scars marked a meandering path leading from *Fini Terre.* Throughout the summer Ty and the guides and wranglers had kept a sharp watch, with bear sightings few and distant.

But the grizzly would be on the move again, and ill with the moods of the coming winter sleep. If one had chosen a den on *Fini Terre,* as it vacillated in and out of this dormant time, waking for periods from what was not true hibernation, it would be even more dangerous. Ty made a mental note to check the lower meadow.

"It's probably nothing, just Shadow being Shadow." Ca-sually, not wanting to alarm her unduly, he added, "Until we know for certain, it might be better if I rode the lower pas-ture."

"Sure. Whatever you say." Considering the subject closed, noting the papers he held, Merrill scraped back a chair and dropped into it. Nodding toward the crumpled stack, she asked, "How does the book go? Making progress?"

She'd been surprised, and yet not, when in one of their games of twenty questions, never truly twenty in number, she'd asked and learned that in his winter exile, Tynan O'Hara was a writer. An author, to be exact, of no little success.

As Patrick O'Hara he wrote mysteries with a Western theme, and was better than good. She had, in fact, read several in the past. She'd been reading one on the evening of their first real talk, and more since.

After all, she asked herself now as he scowled down at a particular page, why should she be surprised? He was articulate, educated, he told a story concisely and clearly. That had been evident from the beginning, and demonstrated clearly when he related the story of how Shadow came to be with him. With the same skill, his books were a meticulous weaving of fact and fiction, with intriguing characters a part of the warp and woof, holding them together.

Even with their twenty questions, neither had ever pried deeper than the other was willing to allow. They'd touched only briefly on her work with The Black Watch. In vague terms she'd described the good parts, the successes, and glossed over the failures and the tragedy. The worst of which had driven her into the depression that ultimately led her to *Fini Terre*. Land's End.

"Progress!" Ty growled, drawing her from digression and back to the question. "If you call painting the hero into a corner and leaving him no reasonable escape, then, yes, I've made great progress." He tossed the pages on the table, letting them scatter as they would. "I thought a change of scene would help."

That explained this uncustomary venturing from his lair. "No good?"

"Not in the least."

"Cabin fever." Merrill made a glaring diagnosis. She'd volunteered to ride fence while he worked out particular literary problem. Since he kept only horses and no cattle through the winter, riding fence was simply a matter of inspection and repair of damage done by weather and wild animals. After a crash course in what to look for and what to do if she found anything out of the ordinary, the job had become hers.

"What you need is a ride to the shack," she declared, coming promptly to the natural solution. "The fresh air would revive any mind and imagination."

Gathering the scattered papers up with sweep of his arm, with no concern for their order, Ty stacked them away. "You're right. What I need is a change. A good hard gallop and a day out of doors should cure what ails me."

"Want some company?" Merrill stared down at her hands, feigning interest in a chipped nail. She'd seen little of Ty lately, while she rode fence and he barricaded himself in his lair. Over the course of days, she'd missed him and didn't want him to see her disappointment if he preferred to ride alone.

Standing by his chair, his hand gripping the back of it, Ty looked down at her. Her expression was almost hidden by the mass of her hair. Dear heaven she had beautiful hair. Bright as sunlight on a summer day. If he breathed deeply, he could almost catch the scent of it, wild flowers, summer flowers, threading through the clinging purity of the autumn air.

Wild flowers and Merrill and sunlight. The words haunted him. The picture they painted drove him mad. Cabin fever was the least of his problems.

"Sure," he heard himself saying. "Come along."

Wise move, O'Hara, he chastised himself, nothing like taking your problem on a quest to solve your problem. To compound the difficulty he added, "The way to the shack will be impassable soon, so why not more than a ride. How about one last fling?"

"Define fling." Merrill had forsaken the study of her nails, trading it for a close inspection of Ty. He looked less than overjoyed at the prospect of a ride or her company. Hardly a mood for a fling, whatever his definition.

"A picnic." Ty relaxed the death grip that threatened the slats of the chair, improvising as he went. "Bread, cheese, a good red wine. Along the way we can swing by the lower pasture to check out the tracks and see if we can rein Shadow in."

"A long ride," Merrill commented.

Like cabin fever, a long ride was the least of his troubles. "In a hurry?"

"Of course not."

"Then it's settled. The meadow, then the shack. If we run late, no problem. The moon is full and can light our way home."

If he'd said it through gritted teeth, the invitation couldn't be more stern. "Thanks," Merrill worked at sounding non-chalant. "But I'd better take a rain check. I just remembered some things I should do, and you probably need the time alone more than you need company."

"I've been alone. For days. Weeks. Months." Ty bit back a curse. None of the blame for his angry mood should fall on her. It wasn't her fault that she distracted him, that he watched her when she was near, and thought of her when she wasn't.

It wasn't her fault she was desirable and tempting and he'd been without a woman for so long. Nor that the hero of the book in progress couldn't think any clearer than his creator. Closing his eyes, shutting the innocent source of his troubles from sight, Ty drew a long hard breath. He wasn't a bull moose, and this wasn't rutting season. Merrill was his guest, and he'd known what he was letting himself in for when he agreed to let her stay.

"Maybe if I'd taken the little blonde up on her invitation," he muttered beneath the breath that rushed from him in a hoarse growl.

He hadn't taken her up on her invitation, and he hadn't responded to her flirtatious advances. As he hadn't so many others over the years. From the first, his policy was that there would be no sexual entanglements, no intimacy greater than friendship between staff and guests. Flirting was fun, the sexual fencing even stimulating, yet he'd never wanted or needed to cross the line. He'd never come close to breaking the rules, until now.

The summer ladies came for a short time. A week or two, scheduled into busy lives, to taste the adventure of the northwest. He, or one of the hands had taken them with family, friends, or lovers, into the wild, to camp, to fish, and to hunt wildlife with cameras. Some developed a strong yen for what they considered the two-legged wildlife of Montana. Dealing with it was part of the job.

Never a difficult task before. But none of them had been so aloof and fascinating. Nor lived under his roof, sharing his mornings and his nights, becoming more than a passing part of his life. His teeth clenched, a muscle at his temple jerked. A growl sounded deep in his throat. "Too much a part."

"Ty?" Understanding neither his words nor his mood, Merrill rose from her chair, touching his arm in concern. When he flinched away, she jerked back, knocking her cup from the table, shattering crockery and spilling the last of her coffee over the floor.

"Ohh, no!" Kneeling in the carnage, she gathered dripping bits and pieces of the cup in her palm. "One of your wonderful Indian pieces." Her fingers were shaking, making the task more difficult. "I shouldn't have disturbed you."

Ignoring shards of broken earthenware and the spreading puddle of coffee, Ty knelt before her. Taking jagged fragments from her, he tossed them on the table. "Leave it."

"I can't." She pulled her hand from his. "I have to clean it up. If I'm careful and find all the pieces, maybe it can be repaired."

"Leave it." The words were firm, his tone quiet. "The cup doesn't matter."

"It was so pretty." With her fingertips she tried to dry the brown liquid spreading over the floor.

Catching her hands in his, holding tightly this time, Ty drew them under his chin. His gaze was blue fire, riveting hers. "Leave the cup, leave the coffee. All that's needed is a broom and a mop."

"But..."

"But nothing," he interrupted her lament. "I'll get another cup. I'll get ten, if I want them. And it's guaranteed each will be as pretty."

"Guaranteed?" There was the shimmer of remorse in her eyes.

"Scout's honor."

"You aren't just making this up?"

"Hey, do you think this is the first cup that's been broken here? Do you flatter yourself that smashing dishes is a privilege reserved for you and this is the last replacement Tomas will ever make for me? It isn't, by a long shot, in every case."

"Then why did you use the tin before I came?"

"To save wear and tear, like this, on my knees," he shot back.

She tried a smile and couldn't pull it off. She'd seen Tomas's name on pieces of pottery before. A collection of his work was more than simple earthenware, or table settings. Ty spoke of the potter as a friend. But even if the cup could be replaced, it didn't change what she'd done. "I was careless and clumsy."

"And I'm a grouchy idiot." He kissed her knuckles and chuckled. "With wet knees. Do you think my brew is strong enough to dissolve denim?"

"Oh no. It's…" The lie hovered on the tip of her tongue and was no more successful than her smile. A weak version of the truth prevailed. "It's very strong."

Ty's roar of laughter took her off guard, even as it laid her doubts to rest. Gathering her hands closer, he asked, "So, do we kneel here in the stuff, at loggerheads all day? Or do we find a way to resolve this? What do you suggest?"

"A truce." Merrill proposed succinctly, her hands returning the pressure of his, eyes dark and bright with unshed tears blinked away.

In a familiar habit, Ty cocked a brow at her. "We were at war?"

"A Mexican standoff."

"Near enough. So, as I asked, how do we resolve it?"

This time the smile worked. A little lopsided, a little unsteady. "I sweep, you mop. Or, if you prefer," taking her hand from his, she tapped a finger dead center of his chest, "you mop, I sweep."

"In case you haven't noticed, sweetheart, it's the same in either order," Ty drawled.

"So?" She threw him the look a child might, denying she was filching cookies when her hand was buried in the cookie jar. "What do we have here, another Mexican standoff?"

"With wet knees? I don't think so." Ty climbed to his feet and brought Merrill with him. "I'll mop the floor, *you* sweep."

"That's what I said."

"Twice, dammit." There was no sting in the rare profanity. A silly moment had lightened a bad mood, if not easing the cause.

While she went for the broom, Ty scooped up the shattered parts of the cup, and with a clutch of paper towels soaked up the rest.

"You cheated!" Broom in hand, with nothing to sweep, Merrill leaned on the wooden handle.

"I mopped." Giving the floor one last swipe, he stood to inspect his handiwork. "You didn't say in what order we would perform our duties, nor how."

"Does this mean you make a better Mexican than I."

"That, I would say, is strictly a matter of opinion." He was no more successful with the innocent act than she had been. "Like to go for two out of three?"

"Heaven forbid!" Merrill shuddered. "Your supply of cups couldn't stand it."

"Guess not." He dropped the towels and the remains of the cup in the trash. "Are you up for another challenge?"

She was wary. Stacking her hands one over the other on the broom, she leaned her chin on them and regarded him through narrowed eyes.

"Afraid you'll lose?" he taunted.

"How can I be when I have no idea what you're suggesting?" Suspicion ran rampant.

"Nothing major." Folding his arms over his chest, despite his words, Ty assumed a challenging stance.

A dare. Merrill had never been very good at backing away from a dare. "What's the deal, and what are the odds?"

"The picnic. I quit struggling with a story line that's going nowhere at the moment, you forget about the chores that were suddenly so urgent, and we go." He crossed the kitchen to stand before her. The wildflower scent of her drifted to him, stirring a tenacious flame. "The odds are even."

"Even, huh? What are the stakes?"

"Nothing major there either. The first one changed and dressed gets to choose the wine."

"What about the loser?" She straightened to look up at him, accepting his challenge. "What price does he pay?"

"She, Short Bear. *She.*" His grin was smug. "What will be the loser's penalty?" A fingertip traced the line of her throat, lingered long at the tiny well at its base, measuring the strong and steady beat of her heart. His denim clad shoulders lifted in a shrug. "I haven't decided."

"Neither have I," she shot back at him.

"Cocky! I like that. But you have to win first." He backed away. With a sweep of his arm, he gave her the lead and the advantage. "Win or lose, is it a deal?"

Merrill very carefully leaned the broom against the wall. With her chin tilting a regal inch, she refused to shy away from the burning intensity beneath the laughter. Her chin lifted another degree. "You're on, O'Hara."

"You're quiet."

Her voice was low. A ripple, drawing him from the peaceful atmosphere of the shack. Ty looked up from his study of his tin cup and the dark, red wine. "Does that mean that I'm normally a chatterbox?"

Merrill broke a crust of bread from the half eaten loaf and tossed it to Shadow who lurched from his comfortable place by the hearth to catch it in mid-arc. Teeth snapping with the strength of a steel trap, in one swallow the wolf gulped down the bread. Then, plainly exhausted by the long day of tracking he dropped heavily on the floor again. Muzzle resting on paws, his ice blue eyes flicking from Ty to Merrill, half dozing, he waited for the next morsel with the patience of his kind.

"It means," she said precisely, shaking crumbs from her fingers as she made her point, "I expected you would gloat."

"I got to choose the wine." Raising his cup, he toasted her with it. "What more could I want?"

"The winner's pound of flesh."

"Ahh, yes, there is that." He wanted more than that, much more. With exaggerated indifference Ty picked up a sliver of cheese and added it to Shadow's treats. The wolf lurched, snapped, gulped, and flopped in place to resume his sleepy watch.

"Well?" Merrill prodded.

"I haven't decided. But there's time, the evening is young and there's more wine." Hefting the dusty bottle from its place of honor dead center of the blanket spread over the floor, he refilled her cup and his own.

"You like keeping me in suspense, don't you? Val warned me that you have an abominable obstinate streak, even for an Irishman."

"Of course I have. How can I deny it?" Setting his wine aside he leaned back on the blanket, propping his head on a fist. With his free hand he stroked her arm from elbow to shoulder and back again. "Look how firm I stood and how abominably obstinate I was about you."

She laughed. A small, quiet laugh. "Folded like a crooked prize-fighter."

"Always have, always will, when Val and Patience are concerned. After the expected token resistance."

"You thought I was a man."

"Not for long."

"I expected you to send me packing the first day."

His hand wandered to her shoulder again, his fingers tangling in a loosened strand of her hair. "So did I."

Merrill sighed and relaxed. It was difficult to stay wary

when his touch was pleasing, the room tranquil. Tonight the fire held no demons. "You're a softy, Tynan O'Hara. You've fought battles and wars, hunted men and animals. Along the way from there to here, you've hurt and been hurt. But deep down, beneath the armor, you're a softy.

"That's it, isn't it?" Merrill asked the question that answered a question. "The reason behind *Fini Terre,* for Montana. Val calls this your journey's end. When the blood and the killing became too much, you found your place here."

"*Fini Terre,* a coward's hideaway?" he suggested softly. His fingers coiled once more in her hair, then slipped away as he waited for her response.

"*Fini Terre,* the end of a journey for peace. A wise man's paradise." She touched his shoulder as he'd touched hers, feeling the restrained power of a strong man, remembering his gentle compassion. "A man who is anything but a coward."

"You're sure of that, are you?"

Merrill nodded once, a slight tilt of her head that could've been lost in shadows left untouched by the flickering light of the lantern and the fire. "As sure as I am of anything. No," she said with subdued fervor. "Surer than I am of anything.

"Val has told me about her family." On an evening when the memory of a mission gone wrong was too much. When grief for the young, dark haired, dark eyed, hostages of a small, petty war had been too raw. When guilt that she hadn't saved the children—as she'd been sent to do—had been too devastating.

The doorbell had rung and Merrill had forced herself to answer. Valentina O'Hara, never more than an acquaintance, but once a fellow agent, waited on the doorstep. Waited to become her friend.

She came to talk. Merrill must listen, must hear.

And talk she did, through the night, into dawn. Sense, common sense, nonsense. Fact, fiction. Black, white, gray. She talked of Simon and The Watch, of success and failure, triumph and tragedy. Of coping. She spoke of life and death. She spoke of love and families. Merrill's. Hers.

Somewhere in the darkest depths of that night, Merrill had been drawn from the brink of emotional destruction. Before Valentina was done she had taken the first tottering steps on the long, painfully slow path to recovery. By dawn she was more than half in love with the idea of the O'Haras. A family, not an extension of the military.

"Keegan and Mavis, parents straight out of a lovely, fun filled fairy tale." Her expression grew wistful as she began the roll call. "Quiet, scholarly, brave Patience. Logical Kieran, jack-of-all-trades and master of all, for whom recognizing the impossible is not an option. Dashing, daring Devlin with a wicked grin, a daredevil's soul, and a talent for making both engines and women purr."

"Then Tynan. Reclusive Tynan," he filled in as she fell silent. "Obstinate, even for an Irishman."

The fire crackled, a log collapsed. But there were no voices in the sound crying out to her. No children danced in fiery death.

This was Montana. And Tynan.

"Tynan." Continuing, she dismissed his simplistic summary of himself. "A soldier, with medals for honor and valor and for his wounds hidden away. A gifted hunter who found the hunt—the blood, the death—abhorrent. For whom the killing of animals for pure sport became too much."

Pausing, she recalled the single, most powerful element of Valentina's argument, then Simon's, convincing her that it was here in Montana, here on *Fini Terre,* that she would regain her perspective, her self respect, and her strength. Here, with this man. "Tynan, wisest of the O'Haras. Rancher at heart, philosopher in his soul. Idealist with the courage of his convictions."

"Some would say bleeding heart," he said.

Some had.

"Because you've chosen to hunt with a camera and fishing rod, rather than a gun?"

"Something like that." It hadn't been that simple, but the explanation sufficed.

The fire blazed hotter. A rumble sounded deep in Shadow's throat. As the wolf crawled on his belly an inch further from the heat, an inch closer to Merrill, she set her wine aside to lay the last of her bread and cheese within reach of the furry muzzle.

"I saw a book of photographs," she said as the repast disappeared. "I didn't mean to snoop and I didn't think you'd mind."

"No problem. I make and publish one each season. A sort of album for those who've been here. They each choose a selection of their better photographs. Sometimes of their fishing trophies. These are submitted to a professional photographer who makes the final selections and arranges them in orderly sequence. This year's book will be mailed in time for Christmas."

"A tangible memory of what, for many, was a first in a lifetime adventure."

"I hope so. The kids are the best, the most fun. Shadow usually chooses one as his special person. Someone he senses is troubled. This past summer it was a young girl who lost her sight in an auto accident. She was deathly afraid of animals and had refused a guide dog. After a week she was riding. By the end of the second week, she was eager to get home to set in motion the procedures for acquiring a dog.

"Some of the best photographs this year were hers. Someone was always willing to talk her through a shot, explaining where to focus, the position of the sun and the shadows in relation to whatever animal we encountered. Perhaps it was the keenness of her hearing, or some sixth sense, but she seemed to know how long an animal would stand and when it would bolt. In a way it wasn't a surprise when she became adept at fly casting."

Pausing in his long discourse, he smiled at the pleasant memory. "There are other yearbooks, if you'd like to see them."

"I would. The one I've seen is amazing."

"Even more amazing, when you realize these are amateur

photographers. With a short course of instruction from a trained photographer at the first of their stay, but amateurs still.''

''Modern pioneers going into the wild with trusty camera or fly rod in their scabbards rather than weapons.''

''There are rifles and handguns,'' Ty explained. ''Don't kid yourself about that. Only a fool would venture into the un-populated areas without protection. We can't always predict what we'll run into. A bull moose in rutting season, a rattler, a grizzly with cubs, which do you think would welcome any intrusion?''

''None of the above.''

''Exactly. It isn't rutting season, rattlers have gone to ground, but the grizzly is unpredictable. Go prepared. Expect the unexpected.'' With a two fingered stroke of her cheek, he turned her face to him. ''At the first sign of tracks even re-motely like those we found down by the lower meadow, move cautiously, but move. We have a grizzly on our range. I think a male from the signs. But a he-bear readying for winter sleep or awakened, as they often are, by hunger can be vicious.''

''Worse than a mother with cubs?'' The heat of his touch lingered, a warm radiance that transcended the blazing fire.

Ty's mouth quirked in a grim smile. ''Let's just say I wouldn't want to be the one making the comparison.''

''It's always worse when there are little ones.'' A chilling memory leached every vestige of comforting warmth as she turned again to stare into the fire. ''Little ones,'' her voice broke hoarsely, ''of any kind.''

''I know, sweetheart, I know.'' Ignoring the swift turn of her head and the sear of her probing look, he straightened and shifted, and drew her back against him. When she would have struggled out of his embrace, he quieted her with a single word. ''Stay.'' Then another. ''Please.''

She had no defenses against him. No deaf ear to turn to the tenderness in his voice. No armor to repel the delight of his soothing touch. His fingers were magic, kneading away the mounting tension as his murmuring tones calmed her.

"I know. Santiago," he said her name gruffly. "First in, last out. Speaking the native tongue, becoming one of them. Too close." A bitter accusation. "Too close. Simon shouldn't ask it of you."

Her fingers closing over his wrist stopped him. But she made no effort to move away. "What I do," she whispered, "what I've done, I did because I wanted it. Simon has never once asked more of me than I was willing to give. The last," her grip grew tighter, harder, "the last was my mistake. I waited too long, trusted foolishly, guessed wrong."

She spoke the cost in an unforgiving undertone. "The children paid."

"You made no mistake, Santiago." He took his wrist carefully from her grip. His fingers resumed their questing strokes, easing taut muscles of her neck and shoulders. "Ramon Guiterrez is a dime a dozen crook. A slimy son of a bitch who stumbled on a bit of power, but hasn't a clue to the meaning of honor. He never intended to let the children go. They were destined for death the minute he took them hostage."

Merrill shook her head violently. "A kind lie can't resolve my guilt or bring back the children."

His fingers drove into the tender flesh above her collarbone as if he would shake her and make her listen. "I'm not being kind. What I've said is the truth, not a lie."

"You can't know that!"

His nails scored her skin. Tomorrow he would be sorry, tonight he was only intent that she listen and believe. "I can know. I do know. I was there. When Guiterrez was unimportant slime instead of important slime, I was there."

Merrill would have turned then, to see the look on his face. He wouldn't allow it. "I don't understand."

"What's to understand?"

"You were there, years ago?" Recalling Valentina's tale of the family's wandering, of studying and learning, their unorthodox education gleaned from so many lands, so many cultures, on a guess she said, "But first, as a child."

Though she couldn't see, he nodded. "Then as a man."

"For Simon?" An astonishing concept, but it was, for Merrill, the logical conclusion.

"For myself."

In a startled moment she didn't understand, then his oblique point was clear. "You were a mercenary?"

"Once." The admission was terse. "For a while."

"You wouldn't. You couldn't."

"There were reasons." Realizing how cruelly he held her, he eased the force of his grip, but didn't release her.

"Ramon Guiterrez."

The nod again. "We were friends." A wry smile drew down his mouth as he plucked a pin from her bound hair. "I thought he needed me." Another pin slid away. "What he needed was a fool in a uniform."

"The boy who had been your friend had become the slimy son of a bitch."

Ty laughed then, bitterly. She had a way of cutting to the heart of the matter. "A lying, slimy son of a bitch."

"Right."

The last pin fell. The coil at her nape tumbled down her back. "Are we done with this, Santiago? Do you believe me when I give you my word that nothing could have saved the children?"

"I believe you." And she did. But nothing could ease the hurt of being fooled, or the grief. "Now I understand why Valentina was so certain you could help me."

"I suspect she planned for it to go both ways. Misery loves company, but let's not be miserable for a while." His hands glided the length of her hair, lingered, then fell away. Drawing a long breath, Ty moved away, he moved on. "We have some wine to finish and a toast to make."

When the last of the 'good red wine' trickled into her cup, he touched its rim with his. "To better days."

"In time." For the first time in a long while, Merrill was sure they would come.

Ty regarded his cup and moved on again. "A good wine deserves better days as well."

"Fine goblets, misshapen tin, flavor's the same to any but a connoisseur."

"But there's more to wine than mere flavor. For anyone." His gaze met hers, holding, mesmerizing. "It should be seen, as a beautiful woman should be seen. It's bouquet savored, as her fragrance should be. It's taste cherished as her kisses must."

As the day had fallen beyond twilight, the single lantern had burned low and guttered out. There was only the dying fire to light the last of their simple banquet. The errant desires the ride might have quenched had been kindled and rekindled many times over by what he saw in her face in the soft, lazy play of the flames.

There were times when she looked into the fire and he saw things that made him want to console and comfort her. And times, like now, when she looked at him, her mouth tender, her eyes luminous, and he wanted more. Much more.

Beyond the shack, a full moon rode the crest of the horizon. A brilliant beacon, as he'd promised, to lead them home. The horses, cropping with innate patience, had begun to stir fretfully. Rested from his chase of the meandering bear, Shadow rose, pacing before the glass doors, ready to run, to hunt again, to howl with his genera at the night.

"We should go."

Merrill nodded, but made no more effort to rise than he.

"But first." Taking her wine from her, putting it aside with his, he let the last of his thought trail away as he cupped his palm at the side of her throat. His thumb rested easily over the pulsing hollow, his fingers fit the curve of her nape, teasing the silky tangle that fell over his wrist in a fall of molten gold.

"But first?" she asked as he drew her closer.

"I should collect my wager."

"Then you've decided my fate."

"I've decided."

"And?" He was so close, his lips nearly brushed hers. The clean familiar scent of him tantalized and beguiled as he took her in his arms.

"And this," he whispered as his lips touched hers.

He meant to keep it brief, a teasing penance, the victor collecting his reward. But something in her, the quiet need in the caress of her fingers tangling in his hair, the soft yielding of her mouth, drawing him nearer, holding him closer. She was too sweet. Dear heaven! Too sweet to tease.

The beat of his heart roughened in answer to the enchanting pleasure of her yielding, his kiss deepening, even as his mind said no. Slowly, with the yearning of a man too long alone, his mouth gentled on hers, and slowly he drew away. Looking down at her he knew he wanted her more than he'd wanted anyone and anything. But she was too vulnerable, the emotion in her shadowed eyes too naked.

He'd never known that desire could be gentle and tender. Nor that passion could be patient.

Bringing her back to him, tucking her head against his throat, with his lips a quiet caress against her forehead, he held her close to the calming beat of his heart. From some unfathomable well of wisdom came the certainty that out of gentleness and tenderness desire would flourish and grow richer. Out of patience, passion would become its own reward.

There would come a day when they would make love, must make love. But not yet. Not this day. Tilting her head back, he looked long into the dreamy softness his kiss had awakened in her, and felt a quiet contentment.

"One day," he spoke his thoughts as his lips brushed hers in one last kiss. Putting her from him with a tenderness he'd never known was in him, in a promise left unspoken, he traced the softness of her mouth with a fingertip. "But not this day."

Smiling ruefully, his hands falling away from her, he murmured, "Let's go home, sweetheart."

Five

The door banged at Ty's back as he stamped into the kitchen and tossed his hat and then his jacket aside. Traces of snow that had fallen in the night still clung to toes and heels, and the edge of his jeans. Dusting it away, he straightened, ruffled a stubborn flake or two from the ends of his hair as it curled over his shirt, then drew a long grateful breath.

The kitchen was a maze of intriguing fragrances. Freshly baked loaves of bread cooled on a rack by the stove. Beside them sat an apple pie made from dried fruit sent from Alabama by Matilda Prescott, then shared by Cora Franklin. From a pot simmering on a burner wafted scents of lemon, exotic spices and tea. An exquisite feast for the senses.

A mug waited within reach. Merrill's anticipation that he would need something to quell the chilled numbness left by the cold.

"You've died and gone to heaven, O'Hara," he murmured. "What else could feel and smell like this."

Kicking his boots aside, and pouring the fragrant tea all in one motion, he padded in stocking feet to the great room. Leaning against the doorjamb, as the heat of the fire reached out to him and the tea worked its magic, he watched the source of this pleasant welcome.

She sat before the fire, slippered feet just touching the floor, a box on the sofa beside her, notebook and papers in hand. Her head was bent, her attention focused on some painstaking task. There was quiet purpose in what she did, and concentration so absolute she was completely unaware that he watched. Or that Shadow raised his head from her foot in silent greeting.

Absently she reached for her own mug, missing on the first try when she didn't look up from her work. More successful the second time, she brought it nearly to her lips, paused, looked to her left at a stack of paper, then swiftly to her right at another. In a sudden quickening of interest, or the rush of a thought, the tea was left forgotten and untasted, and the mug set aside. Drawing a pencil from the ribbon that held a disheveled topknot, she scribbled on a pad, tapped the pen against her cheek, then scribbled again.

The pattern was repeated twice more, each of these times with the tea not put aside and forgotten. On the third, she paused in mid scribble. For an endless instant she didn't move. Then, her breasts rising in a breath deeply drawn and slowly released, without turning, she murmured, "You smell of fresh air."

"Do I?" His voice was husky from the chill, from the constant singsong chant his horse liked. From things he wasn't ready to deal with.

Her head tilted down a degree. A tiny nod. "And horses, and leather, and woodsmoke."

And an underlying scent that was his alone, clean and woodsy, and more seductive than any perfumer could create.

"I made a fire for a short break down by the lower meadow." He explained the woodsmoke that would cling stubbornly to him until he washed it away.

There was a frisson of alarm in her, betrayed only by the thread of it in her voice. "You were in the lower meadow?"

"For a while." He heard the concern and cursed himself for causing it. "I'm here now."

"Yes," she said simply, the moment of tension easing. Laying aside the pad and the pen, she turned to him, at last, her face alight. A look he waited for each day.

"Ty." There was genuine pleasure in her voice, as the sight of him and the sound of his name in the stillness lifted her heart. "You're early."

"Only a little." In the background soft music played. Romantic classics, Jamie McLachlan and his piano, at his best, reproduced in compact disc. The perfect accompaniment for the warmth and balm of homecoming. Perfect for this vision of her.

"I didn't hear you come in." Her look moved over him, noting the glitter of melted snow clinging to the tips of his hair, the darkening of chilled flesh drawn taut over craggy cheekbones making his eyes, and their hidden thoughts, that much more intriguing. "How..." Hesitating, refusing to ponder the nature of those thoughts, she regrouped, gathering her scattered wits. "How long have you been standing there?"

"Long enough."

"How long is that?" Her eyes were brighter, her cheeks more flushed.

"Long enough to see that you're quite engrossed in what you're doing. A herd of buffalo could stampede through here and you wouldn't have noticed," he drawled as he pushed away from the door and crossed to the fire. Bracing one arm on the mantel, he nodded toward the box and the neat stacks. "What have you found that's so interesting?"

She glanced down at her work, the color of her cheeks deepening, growing more lovely. "These." Gathering up a handful, she showed him what had prompted the sparkle of excitement. "They were in the cabinet by your music collection. Photographs, hundreds of them. So arresting, so...so..." Defeated, she abandoned her search for the perfect word. "I couldn't *not* look at them."

Shuffling through a stack, drawing out one that pleased her

most particularly, she held it up for his inspection. "These are yours, aren't they? You took them."

There was no mistaking the old box, nor its contents. "They're mine." Setting his tea on the mantel, he took the photograph from her, identified it and returned it. "This is one of many taken over the years.

"My father has a passing interest in photography." He almost laughed aloud at the understatement. There was very little that didn't interest Keegan O'Hara. And any interest, passing or not, was only a step below obsession. "When the five of us were small and traveling the world, he encouraged us to record and remember what we saw."

"With cameras."

"Can you imagine it? Five little O'Haras dashing about, cameras in hand, out to see and conquer the world. At mother's suggestion some of us kept journals or diaries of our travels. One didn't."

"Not Devlin's style?" she ventured, gleaning the assumption from Valentina's family descriptions. She couldn't conceive of the family's boldest venturer keeping either.

"Hardly. He'd rather climb a mountain of ice, or surf with sharks. In fact, he'd rather do most anything, than keep a journal. He was terrific with a camera, though." Chuckling he added, "Kieran compromised by keeping his in lists on whatever scraps of paper were handy. We were always finding them strewn over the house, the maison, the casa, or whatever our lodgings were called, in whatever country.

"My favorite was at our home base on the Chesapeake. It read something like this—'saw a bird, patched a sail, slayed a dragon, kissed a girl, I think I liked it. No, I'm sure I liked it.'"

"And I'm sure he was a while living that one down," Merrill suggested, amused.

"There was more. With Kieran," Ty explained, "there was always more. Lists within lists, detailed description and explanations. This time they were of the bird, in a running column. A discourse and analysis of wind currents, their effect on sailing, in a running column. An explanation that the lizard frightened the girl and made her cry. How he caught it and put it in his pocket to release somewhere else.''

There was laughter in the look that met hers. ''Do I have to tell you the girl, the kiss, and why a twelve-year-old would like it received the same descriptive attention as the bird and the wind?''

Her smile grew wistful as she imagined the wonder and delight of a young boy, his voice just sliding into bass, analyzing his first kiss. ''In running columns, no doubt.''

''Exactly.'' Ty smiled as well. ''The last got a bit graphic for Mother. Body responses and such, down to the last increment. But she never said a word.''

''And your dad?''

''Keegan O'Hara was never one to squelch literary ingenuity, of any sort. His one suggestion was that, in deference to the tender ages of our sisters, Kieran should be a tad more careful with such lists in the future.''

''Keegan O'Hara, diplomat, scholar, and a gentleman.''

Ty took up his tea, sipped, and set it aside again. ''Heart and soul.''

''Was it his influence that led you to make *Fini Terre* into what it is?''

''In that his influence made me what and who I am, yes. In that he is, in part, responsible for the skills I took into the world, yes. Beyond that...'' Pausing he turned to the windows, to the mountains rising like gleaming towers to touch the horizon. ''Beyond that, what you see, is my responsibility, my choice. Foibles and merits, alike, rest precisely at my door.''

''You must admit, given the country, what you do at *Fini Terre* is an unusual concept.'' She chose another photograph to make her point.

''Unusual in that it isn't geared for hunters?'' He barely noticed her nod. ''I tried that for a year or so. Then I realized that I was perpetuating the things I most wanted to leave behind. From there it wasn't a stretch to think that there were others out there like me. People who want to hunt with something other than bullets. Who wanted to experience the land, but would leave the wildlife as they found it.''

"You tailored *Fini Terre* to meet a need." A stack of photographs threatened to topple over. Catching it, she restacked it neatly. "Along the way, returning to the camera yourself."

Ty shrugged, straining the supple flannel of his work shirt. "The summer people get a kick out of seeing a cowboy behind a camera. They figure that for the most part we're on the front end."

"What I see here is more than a cowboy entertaining summer people," she declared, tapping a stack. "I'm far from an expert, but I know when something is well done. When it's startling and memorable."

"They were never meant to be taken seriously. Just part of the fun."

"The end product of fun, in this case, is marvelous. You turn your guest's photos into books. A private printing as a lasting memento. But have you ever considered doing the same with your own? Putting them in order, a flowing sequence, writing a caption for each. Something that prompted you to take the picture. What you feel when you look at it."

She hadn't asked who wrote the most interesting journal of the O'Haras's travels. Or which had a way with words. There was no need. Her gaze settled on Ty, seeing a boy only a little younger than his two brothers, only a little older than his sisters. A boy with a way with the camera as well as words. "There's a book here, and you could find a publisher, I'm sure of it."

Tossing a picture back to the box, he said succinctly, "There isn't a book here, Santiago. Not one for the public market, but thanks for the confidence."

"Are you angry that I dragged them out? Am I poking my nose where it shouldn't go?" She couldn't think of a reason, but it occurred to her that he might not want her to see them. "Have I intruded again?"

Going to sit by her side on the sofa, he took her hands in his, as he might a troubled child. "You haven't intruded and

I'm not angry. You aren't poking your nose where it shouldn't go. Drag the box any damn place you wish. If I cared that you would see them, if they were some great dark secret, they would have been under lock and key.''

"Then do you mind if I put them in order, into a scrapbook. Something your summer people might enjoy." She tried to be casual, but failed mightily. "It would be something to amuse myself with while I'm cooped up here."

"Something instead of baking bread and pies, and making tea?" Yesterday it was Bear Sign, the doughnut-like sweet every cowboy loved. The day before, chili, the likes of which he'd never enjoyed. The day before that, the barn had been cleaned. He'd asked her to stay close while there were real bear signs about the range. No taxing chore when the weather was mean and nasty. But in these mellow days of the mildest Montana winter in history, a real cause for going stir crazy.

"A change of pace," she said. "To pass the time in the afternoons and evenings."

Her words were innocent, the sting of guilt they elicited unintentional. Yet they went straight to his conscience. He'd tried to convince himself that it was for the book that he shut himself away from her. That it was going so well that he spent his late afternoons and evenings slaving over a red hot computer. But if he were truthful, which in the end was the only way he knew to be, the book was an excuse. A way of not dealing with Merrill and the desires and passions she stirred in him. He wondered if this flurry of cooking and cleaning, was her panacea for a troublesome libido as well.

God help him, the aching hunger was his constant companion. He had only to look at her, or hear her voice, or feel the brush of her hand against his, and it was there. The need, the longing. A thirst only she could quench. It was in him now, like a demon, a sweet demon, driving him mad.

"Make what you like of the photos," he heard himself say in a voice unlike his own. "But for now, put them aside. I have something to show you."

At her look of askance, in a sudden rush of impatience, he

took the pad and pen from her and pitched it aside. "Are you up to cross-country skiing."

"I beg your pardon?" She was looking at him as if he'd lost his mind, and he wasn't certain that he hadn't.

"Cross country skiing," he repeated each word with exaggerated care. "Can you?"

"Of course." She was puzzled at the mercuric change in him. "But why?"

"Because I have something to show you." Relenting in his strange mood, he admitted a truth he hadn't faced until now. "Because it's a good day for it, and the reason I came home early."

"You want to go skiing?" She was having difficulty with this about-face in a man normally as steady as Ty. "What about the bear?"

"There's been no sign of him for a week. He's moved on, or returned to sleep." As he stood, he took her with him. When she swayed against him, unbalanced by the suddenness of his move, the easiest thing to do was to put his arms around her, to hold her. The hardest was to let her go. "Easy there," he muttered as he set her from him. "Are you okay?"

"I'm..." The assurance she intended never reached her mind or her lips as her look collided with his. The fierceness in his stare was startling, stealing rational thought away. A demon rode his shoulder, one that sent him ranging the land until it was time to lock himself away in his lair. A demon they both must face one day. One day soon.

Unsettled by the notion, by his touch, unable to face the fury building like a storm in him, she looked away. "I'm fine."

Ty nodded curtly. "We'll leave when you're ready." He took a step back, putting the safety of distance between them. "Shadow can't go this time. I'll see to the fire and the stove, then take him to the barn. Remember to dress warmly. When you've finished, I'll be waiting outside."

Merrill stared after him long after he'd whistled for the wolf, long after the door closed behind them. "One day," she whispered, as certain the time would come as she was of the next beat of her heart.

Hurrying then to her room, taking down her hair as she went, she dressed for an afternoon in the snow. When she'd finished, combed and groomed and wisely dressed, she found herself lingering by the window, moving the shutter aside. Shadow was nowhere in sight, but Ty was there by the corral, attending a final chore. She watched him in this rare unguarded moment, desire such as she'd seen in him shivering deep inside her.

"One day," she spoke her conviction softly. "One day soon."

The shutter clattered against the wall as she turned from it, hurrying to the day at hand.

"They're magnificent. I've never seen anything more beautiful."

Ty laughed softly at her whispered wonder. "A buffalo is beautiful?" He shook his head as if despairing of her judgment. "Remind me not to be too flattered by any compliment you might give me."

He was only teasing, for they were beautiful, these massive creatures that once roamed the plains in herds so great they were days in passing.

"You don't fool me, Tynan O'Hara," Merrill retorted from her perch in the cluster of rocks high above the meadow where the buffalo grazed. They were the reason Shadow had been denied a run. Ty hadn't wanted the risk of spooking the small herd before she saw them. "You wouldn't have brought me here, it wouldn't even have occurred to you, if you didn't think they were beautiful too."

"Guilty as charged." Easing from one stone to another, careful not to startle the herd, he moved closer to her. Even with the snow, the day was mild. But still cold enough that they should move on soon. Yet he was loath to hurry her as she watched in fascination.

"Look!" She clutched his sleeve, capturing an attention she already commanded. "He's scraping the snow away."

The bull stood with his nose buried in the snow, his great head tossing from side to side, until a patch of grass showed pale green. "He'll do that until he's grazed his fill," Ty told her. "If they haven't moved on by tomorrow, I'll bring down some hay."

"Move on? Where would they move to? For that matter, where did they come from?"

"The Triple C. Carl and Catherine Carlsen keep them pastured in the spring and summer. But since the mountains form a natural basin those of us here give them free range of our unfenced pastures in winter. We keep an eye out for them and notify the Carlsens where they are." Reluctant as he was to take her away, it was time they pushed on.

The buffalo were only part of his afternoon agenda. "The Triple C will be our next stop, if you're up to more skiing."

"The Carlsens, another of your nearest neighbors?"

"Right."

The look she turned on him was filled with pure horror. "Forty miles away."

"That's by the roads." She wore a knit cap that left only her face exposed, he tugged it lower over her forehead. "We go as the crow flies."

She looked at him dubiously, through narrowed eyes. "How far does the crow fly?"

"Five more miles. All of it downhill."

"Of course, that makes sense," she commented dryly. "Forty by the road, five by snow."

With two fingers he tilted her chin. "What's the matter, Santiago? Don't you trust me?"

In a flash the tension between them returned. Both knew his question had little to do with roads or crows flying. Both knew her answer would set the path they would inevitably take.

Beneath a sky that never seemed to end, in this day wrapped in its gown of virginal white, there was stillness as peaceful as a great cathedral, silence as glorious as music. In this great open space, there was no room for lies. "I trust you, O'Hara." Her lashes swept her cheeks, then lifted to reveal her steady golden-brown gaze. "With my life."

Tynan's breath shuddered from him, the breath he hadn't known he held. With the back of his hand he stroked the slope of her cheek, his knuckles tarrying at the corner of her mouth.

In the meadow beneath their perch, the bull snorted and huffed, catching a drift of their scent. One wrong move and the herd would run. Slowly, though the creature couldn't see, yet careful to make no sudden or disturbing gesture, Ty dropped his hand away.

A half grown calf bawled. His mother answered. The bull lowered his head again to snuffle at the snow and lumbered a little distance away. The herd was quiet again. The moment passed.

"We'd better go," Ty said hoarsely, his look still lingering on her face. She'd never been lovelier than with the bright flush drawn to her cheeks by the cold, sharp air; the steady, gold spangled gaze, its sparkle of excitement and delight darkened with desire; her mouth soft and tempting.

It seemed natural that he kiss her. Here in the still, quiet place. A simple brush of his lips against hers. A promise made.

Lifting his head, he found himself drowning in the dark well of her eyes. With a knuckle he followed the path his lips had taken. A memory to keep.

"We'd better go," he heard himself repeating.

Merrill glanced away, a token distancing from a flame that burned too fiercely. "To the Carlsens'."

With a nod, he took up his skis and hers, leading her from the maze of stone that had been their hiding place and into the open field of snow. Kneeling there he strapped on her skis and his. When he straightened, as he towered over her, he knew she had, indeed, trusted him with her life. From the first day to this.

Adjusting his backpack comfortably over his shoulders and

laying a gloved hand on her shoulder, he asked softly, "Ready?"

"Will we see the buffalo again?"

"They'll be around."

"Then, I'm ready."

Ty blazed the way over the last and most difficult part of the trail. He didn't need to look back to know that she followed, believing he would keep her safe. Trusting that he would bring her no harm.

"Well now, if you aren't a sight to gladden my heart, I don't know what is!" She was a big woman. Tall and rangy, and made to seem even bigger by the thick, down coat she wore. Buckets of grain lay scattered where she dropped them as she enveloped Ty in the next best thing to a bear hug. "What brings you here?" She asked in one breath, and in the next turned to Merrill. A work worn hand drawing the smaller woman close. "And who might this pretty little thing be?"

Eyes as green as new grass in spring and dancing with laughter peered from a weathered face wrapped in a scarf topped by a Stetson. "Not one of your sisters, that's for sure. No black Irish in her with eyes like that."

"Don't be disingenuous, Catherine." Ty draped an arm over Merrill's shoulder.

"Disingenuous?" The woman snorted. "The word isn't in my vocabulary, so how could I be."

"Of course it isn't," he drawled. "While you were back East living the life of the rich and famous, it was a word and a condition that completely escaped you. Just as the gossip that *Fini Terre* had a winter lodger escaped you."

Her skiing apparatus left in the barn, Merrill stood between them, a sapling among tall timber. Her head turned back and forth in wonder and amusement at the affectionate badinage. That they were fond of each other was evident. That one would best the other at every opportunity was equally as evident.

"Gossip?" The calloused palm and long elegant fingers

closed tighter over Merrill's. "How in the name of Hades would I hear gossip out here in the middle of nowhere?"

"Had your telephone taken out, did you?" Ty shot back. "Suzy Overmyer didn't see Merrill pass by coming in and never going out? You know, Suzy who sits there practically in the road. Suzy who sees all, hears all, tells all?"

Searching her memory, Merrill remembered a small house separated from the road by a small picket fence. A picturesque setting, with laundry drying in the sun, and a plump, elderly woman sitting in a rocker on the porch. But that was heaven only knew how many miles ago. Another example, as she was discovering today, that in Montana distances were irrelevant.

"Merrill." The striking gaze turned again to her. "An interesting name. I don't suppose anyone has ever called you Merry."

Taken by surprise by what was more astute observation than question, Merrill responded faintly, "Never anyone who knew me."

"Didn't think so." A curt nod tipped the brim of the Stetson. "Despite your tiny size, and as pretty as you are, you don't seem the type for cute names."

Ty laughed and drew Merrill closer to his side. "So speaks Cat Carlsen, the wisest lady I know." Then more formally he said, "Merrill Santiago, meet Catherine C. Carlsen of The Triple C. Cat meet Merrill. Sometimes known as Short Bear, but never, ever Merry."

A twinkle appeared in the cool green eyes. A wide, strong mouth stretched into a stunning grin as both Cat Carlsen's hands enfolded Merrill's briefly, then moved away. "Well, well, he finally remembered his manners. And he's kinda pretty too, isn't he?"

Cat Carlsen didn't wait for an answer, nor did she worry about the spilled grain as she herded them across the yard toward the old, rambling house. "Come in. You must be cold and tired. As I was leaving the house for the feed shed, Carl was putting together a pot of mulled cider. With a splash of brandy it should warm you up nicely."

The woman was a whirlwind, giving neither of them time to accept or decline as she led the way up the steps to the porch. "Carl sprained an ankle a few days ago. Since then, he's tended the house and Casey, while I see to the stock."

"How is Casey?" Ty's hand on Cat's shoulder stopped her before she could open the door.

"Better." The answer came quickly, without reservation. "Much better." For Merrill's benefit she explained, "Casey is our son. He was injured six months ago in a rodeo. He doesn't speak, but he hears and understands." A smile eased the flicker of strain the mention of her son had caused. "He loves company." Patting Merrill's cheek, her smile grew brighter. "Especially the pretty ones."

The door swung wide. A man filled the space as solidly as the door itself. He was tall, taller even than Catherine in his stocking feet. The term bull shouldered came to Merrill's mind, and fit as if it were coined especially for him. The rest of him was lean and spare, a body honed of any excess. His hair was long, black as a starless night. Sharply planed cheekbones would have given his face a cruel cast, were it not for the kindest, soft brown eyes Merrill had ever seen.

This was Carl Carlsen, it had to be, for there was love in the look that lingered on Catherine before it turned to Merrill, then Ty. "Company!" His voice was as soft and kind as his eyes. "What a relief. I heard Cat jabbering out here and was afraid the lonelies had finally gotten to her."

Pointed fingers drilled into his chest, then danced upward to tug his ear. "How can I be lonely with you underfoot all day?" In an aside she said, "Merrill, in case you haven't figured it out, this big galoot is my husband."

For the second time, Merrill's hand was engulfed by a hard, workworn grip. Carl Carlsen held her fingers gently, as his look skimmed over her from top to toe. There was Indian blood flowing strongly in him. She knew from books she'd found in Tynan's library there were eleven tribes in Montana. Ranging from the Blackfeet with its many thousands, to the Cree with less than one. From the local and the look of him, and for no other reason, she would have judged Carl Carlsen to be of the Blackfeet. A nation among the most formidable horsemen of the Northwest Plains.

"Merrill." He bowed formally over her hand, before turning to Ty. Grasping his elbow as Ty did the same, his greeting was deep and pleasant, "It's good to see you again. It's been too long. Casey has missed you. We all have."

He stepped back from the door. Another graceful, gallant bow gestured them inside. "Come in, shed your coats and warm yourselves by the fire."

When Merrill would have shrugged out of the heavy jacket, Carl was there first, sliding it from her and hanging it by the door. "The cider's warm and spicy, but if you'd prefer something else?"

"The cider, please," Merrill was quick to respond. Since coming to Montana she always seemed to have a drink of some sort in her hand. Coffee, tea, wine, now cider. Though she knew it was in part natural hospitality, she knew as well, it was a necessity. A guard against the effects of the cold. "How could I refuse? If it tastes only a tenth as wonderful as it smells, it should be heaven."

Carl limped away, while Cat led them to the fire. The room was spartan, the furnishings minimal and functional. Yet in the clean, spare lines, there was a sophisticated sense of style and comfort. There were paintings on the walls, landscapes and ranch scenes and portraits, in watercolors and oils. And wood carvings scattered about on shelves and tabletops, of waterfowl, wild animals, and horses. Some were crudely done and barely recognizable. Some were perfection in miniature and one almost waited for the blink of an eye or the swish of a tail. The progressive work of one person? Merrill wondered. Or simply a collection of many?

Seeing the direction of her interest, Cat paused in the act of removing her own winter apparel. Tossing the jacket and the Stetson carelessly toward their respective pegs, she came to Merrill's side. "Casey did all of these, the paintings and the carvings." With one hand touching an eagle that needed only

the flutter of a wing to seem real, with the other she tugged
the scarf from her hair. "This was the last one."

"He's amazing." Stopping short, Merrill tried not to stare.
As Cat had drawn the scarf away, the most magnificent mane
of silver and gold tumbled to her waist. It caught the light in
a dazzling display and made a lovely woman all the more
breathtaking and oddly familiar. Struggling to regain her train
of thought, she stroked a faultless wing. "I've seen them like
this, down by the river, catching salmon. Casey's quite tal-
ented."

"Yes, he is." Cat moved on, by unspoken, mutual consent
taking Merrill on a guided tour. "He was riding before he
could walk, and whittling as soon as Carl would trust him with
a knife. The painting came next." She paused before the ren-
dering of a moose. Gangling, ugly. Splendid. "I'd hoped he
would study for a while, then return to the ranch. Maybe build
a studio down by the river."

Merrill said nothing. Intuition telling her that this was a
mother who seldom had the opportunity to speak candidly of
her son.

"There was a scholarship to a prominent art institute,
awarded by the National Association of Indian Artists. He was
eligible because of Carl's tribal ancestry. But it was Casey's
talent that won it."

"When would he have gone." Bits and pieces of masculine
voiced conversation drifted to them, as Carl and Ty settled
down to catch up on the latest happenings on each ranch.
Merrill strolled on, listening to the indistinct hum, thinking,
as time spun out, that Cat Carlsen wouldn't or couldn't answer.

"September," she spoke only a little above a whisper. "He
would have gone in September."

"But the rodeo came first."

Cat nodded, looking at neither Merrill nor the carvings. "He
wanted to prove himself first. He wanted his dad to see that
he could be a champion cowboy as well. Carl didn't think he
should. Tried to convince him it wasn't necessary. Because it

meant so much to Casey, and because I wanted him to be all that he could be, I disagreed.''

And the path of Casey Carlsen's life changed forever. ''Carl doesn't blame you.''

''No, he doesn't. As he sees it, there is no blame.'' Their journey had come full circle to a cluster of chairs gathered before the fire. ''Neither do I. All the factors were weighed, a vote taken and as the majority ruled a decision was made. Casey rode, and he rode well. Then he was injured.'' A shrug of pain barely moved her shoulders. ''But who's to say that if he hadn't ridden, the outcome wouldn't have been worse.''

''So now you deal with what you have, with the best that you have in you.''

''Yes.'' Cat's smile was in place once more. ''We cope, we work, we pray, and each day brings its own rewards.''

In a word and a phrase, Catherine Carlsen spoke volumes of strength, of wisdom. Merrill wondered if she could ever be as strong. Ever as accepting and wise.

''So,'' Carl had risen, as had Ty, waiting to seat them. ''You've had the guided tour.''

''Casey's work is marvelous. I've seen pieces with the mark of his style at Ty's.''

''The wolf and the dove,'' Ty named a most unusual work. ''And the white buffalo. Casey gave them to me. He always said that when the time came, it would be commissioned work that would carry a price tag.'' A look scanned the whole of the room in general, and each piece specifically. ''These come from his heart, and his heart isn't for sale.''

''When the time comes,'' Merrill said softly, sadly.

''It will.'' Carl's tone was not adamant, only resolute, with no need for the excesses of adamancy. ''But enough of that. Come sit close to the fire. I noticed when you came in that you wore no gloves.'' He cast an accusing glance at Ty. ''Your hands must be frozen.''

''Not at all.'' Merrill rushed to Ty's defense as she took the offered chair. ''I'd taken them off just after we skied in.''

"Speaking of skiing," Ty interjected. "We need to be going soon."

"Please don't." Catherine turned her cat's eyes to him. "You've just arrived and you haven't seen Casey. He'd be disappointed if he missed you." To Merrill she explained, "Ty is his most favorite human being in all the world."

"Next to his parents," Ty qualified.

"Maybe," Cat agreed. "But he looks on you as the brother he would have chosen, if there were such choices."

"He'll be awake soon." Carl stood by the fire, a tall silhouette against the dancing flame. "Stay for supper. There's spaghetti on the stove and plenty of it. Make an evening of it, later I'll break out the Sno-Cat. The ride back to *Fini Terre* will give Merrill a chance to see the wonder of a snowy night in Montana moonlight."

"Merrill?" Ty came to stand behind her, his hand rested lightly on her shoulder.

She was dubious, having seen the Sno-Cat in the barn. A heavy machine, like Ty's, that appeared to be the offspring of the mating of a snowmobile and a Caterpillar. A most difficult machine to drive. "What about your ankle?"

Carl looked down at the wrapped and swollen appendage. "No problem. I've been faking so Cat here would have to brave the snow while I lazed around inside."

"Listen to the man," Cat crowed. "He hates being cooped up inside." Turning to Merrill, in a laughing stage whisper she said, "It would be worth a little ache or pain to get him out of the house for a bit. He's been like a moose with a sore dewlap lately."

"You're sure?" Merrill addressed Carl, as he lounged against the mantel.

"I'm sure."

"Then I'd like to stay. I'd like to meet Casey."

"Then it's settled. Now for your long delayed cup of cider." Carl hobbled to a tray on a sideboard, waving away any offers of help as he filled two more heavy mugs. Proving his agility under duress, he made it back to them, with none of the pungent liquid spilled. "A toast," he said as he took up his position by the fire once more. "To a happy evening, and many more."

"To happy evenings," the others murmured in unison.

Setting his mug down with a thud, Ty moved toward the door and his jacket. "Since we're going to stay, I'll see to the animals."

Cat lurched from her chair. "I had forgotten. Ty, there's no need for you to trouble yourself. I can do it."

"I know there's no need, I know you can do it, but it's also no trouble." Ty had already shrugged into his jacket and his cap. "Stay, keep Merrill company. Discover what things you have in common." Giving Cat no more opportunity to argue, he stepped through the door and tramped across the porch.

"I'll see about Casey," Carl announced. As quickly as that, the women were alone, with only the crackle of the fire and the slide and thud of Carl's footsteps down the hall.

The sound faded into silence before Cat turned her gaze from the fire to Merrill. "You've figured it out. There was a moment when I took off the scarf when you felt the familiarity. Now you know."

"I think so."

"You don't think, you know who I am."

Merrill didn't dissemble or pretend. "Cat Carlucci, model, jet-setter. Granddaughter of a Mafia Don, the Godfather. One of the beautiful people. Whose wonderful, glorious golden hair was her trademark."

Cat's gaze returned to the fire. "Some called me whore."

"Yes."

"Some, murderess."

Merrill only nodded.

Six

"It must be strange finding someone like me in Montana. Someone like I used to be," Cat amended quietly. "As strange as it is to have someone recognize me."

"It was a long time ago," Merrill reminded.

Cat studied the younger, smaller woman critically. "You would have been a very young girl when the scandal hit the papers."

"I was twelve, and anxious to be thirteen. My father was a career soldier stationed in the States for the first time in more than three years," Merrill explained. "I loved being back home, I wanted to immerse myself in my own culture. Be a part of it, not an outsider." The dismissing lift of a shoulder, the tightening grip on the arm of her chair betrayed another unhappy part of her childhood. "I was a misfit, struggling not to be."

Cat smiled into the fire, her head bowed. "A not so uncommon phase for an American teen. Most of us cope, in one way or another. We either outgrow the desperation to be part of the crowd, or we change.''

''I was years away from the maturity and understanding that being different wasn't disastrous.'' Merrill didn't elaborate that in her family it was worse. Settling back in her chair, encouraged by Cat's gentle observation, she found it easier to put her family and the disappointment she'd been from her mind. This was ultimately about Catherine Carlucci and how she came to be an indelible influence in the life of an uncertain adolescent.

''But you coped? I think you would always cope, Merrill Santiago.''

''I did, by choosing change. I began by buying the fashion magazines, trying to learn about hair and makeup, and clothing. All of which were low priorities in our home. I hid them under my bed.'' She could smile now at the callow, almost teen, and the secret cache of slickly elegant publications her father branded nonsense. ''Your covers were my favorites. I wanted to look exactly like you. I spent hours pretending I could and would if only I had the right makeup, the right clothes, the right hairstyle.''

An astute gaze considered Merrill again, slowly, thoroughly. ''Not such a great stretch of the imagination in any case. The eyes are different, but the hair is the same, the skin tones.'' Without a modicum of regret she corrected herself. ''The skin tones of my younger days, before Montana.''

Merrill remembered the sophisticated, yet innocent beauty. Six feet tall, rail thin, though shapely, with tawny skin and tawny hair, and eyes like emeralds. Carlucci the cat, every young girl's dream, her allure and celebrity enhanced by mystery. No one knew who she was, or where she came from. But no one cared. All that mattered was that she was young and beautiful, the brightest star. The most desirable, courted by sheiks and princes and movie stars.

There had never been anyone like her. Never one so perfectly suited for the camera. But one day it all ended in tragedy.

A would-be suitor fell from the balcony of her penthouse, taking Catherine Carlucci's bright world with him.

A tabloid was first to reveal her connection with the Mafia. From there rumors escalated. There were whispers of deceit and deception. Of drugs and orgies. Gutter journalism had a field day, feeding off the tragedy of another to fill their own pockets. In a twisted headline and a heartbeat a once heralded beauty became a malevolent weapon. Innocence, sordid. A foolhardy stunt by a silly, lovesick young man became murder.

Carlucci, the glorious, magnificent cat became Catherine Carlucci the criminal, offspring of criminals. Depraved, corrupt, immoral.

Each story was more lurid than the one before. Modeling jobs vanished. No one wanted a fallen idol representing their product. She had become a pariah, yet through it all, she went on with her life, day by day. Proud, beautiful, silent.

Then, on another day, she wasn't there. Catherine, whoever she was, whatever she was, simply disappeared.

The press couldn't find her. Those closest to her, those trusted few who knew where she'd gone, weren't talking.

Without fodder for more rumors, the stories dwindled, died. In less time than it took to destroy the life and reputation of a beautiful young woman, the destructive attention of the unscrupulous turned to newer, fresher tragedy.

Catherine Carlucci was yesterday's sensation. Stale, boring news.

"Twenty years ago." Merrill did some basic arithmetic. "Casey would have gone away to school this fall. That means he had completed high school. That would make him seventeen or eighteen. You came to Montana that long ago?"

Cat nodded.

"Quite a change from your other life."

"Quite."

"Did you miss it? The modeling, the glamour."

"Not for a minute."

"Then you wouldn't go back? You wouldn't have your life as it was?"

A small laugh sounded like a sigh in Cat's throat. "It was never really my life anyway. And never so wonderful and glamorous. Most of what the public saw and read was hype. Not even close to the truth.

"I came from a strict Italian family, with a paternal grandmother from Spain. A little digression in the lineage, to complicate the complicated and pepper the family with a few throwback blondes. Certainly the discipline was nothing to rival a dedicated military family, yet rigid in its own traditions. Contrary to public outcry, my mother had rejected her father and all he stood for. I never knew him. Because I was only seventeen when I began modeling, there were always chaperones. Finally one in particular. Years later, she was still with me.

"None of the romances were real. Can you imagine they could be, with someone who was the epitome of Spanish duennas never more than a touch away? Most of the dates were arranged anyway. The royalty the press made so much of were usually penniless vagabonds looking for the publicity. The sheik was simply an obnoxious old man shopping for an American to add to his harem."

She looked at Merrill with neither anger nor sadness in her expression. "I was a commodity to be marketed. Would you believe I was twenty-one before I had a real date? No arrangement. No duenna."

"Twenty-one? You truly were sheltered."

"Mind-boggling, isn't it? Considering the image projected on camera." Cat laughed. "My father still wanted to choose my suitors. In fact he chose a husband for me. We were to visit once in our parlor, be introduced—with the duenna present, of course. Next would come the ceremony."

"But there was no meeting, no ceremony."

"I went to the rodeo instead."

"And met Carl?"

"I went to scoff, to make fun of the cowboys. Half wild creatures from the uncivilized West. When a bronc dumped Carl on his backside in front of our box, I laughed. He climbed to his feet, dusted himself off, grinned at me and winked. I don't know what caprice made me to do it, but I took a pink heart shaped medallion from my neck and threw it at his feet. He scooped it up, grinned again, and sauntered off to his next ride.''

"He wore your favor," Merrill ventured.

"He still does. He calls it his talisman." There was laughter, again, in Cat's tone at the incongruity of it. Carl, dark, brawny, whipcord tough—and a pink heart. "He keeps it tucked under his shirt.

"He won that day and every day thereafter. Always with my heart lying near his." Her expression grew pensive, thinking, remembering. "After the first day, I went back alone. No date, no duenna. Not an easy thing to accomplish, but I did. On the first day that I returned, he wasn't scheduled to ride and he wasn't there. On the second, as I left the arena, he was waiting. And each day from then on."

There was silence between them, as Cat stepped back into the past and Merrill waited.

With a sigh, a lazy chuckle, and a slow wondering move of her head, sending a wealth of golden, silver streaked locks tumbling over her shoulder, Cat murmured, "He was a bold one. All brash and dash and cocky self-confidence with a quick grin. But he was shy and quiet too. And kind, and thoughtful, and gallant. A mix of so many things, so utterly charming. A man like none I'd ever known."

"You fell in love."

"Madly. Completely. On the first day, with the first grin, the first wink."

"Any regrets?"

"One." There was grief in her voice now, that neither time, nor all Carl's kindness and love could erase. "For the boy who fell from my balcony."

Merrill might have been young, but the story was etched in her memory. "Why was he there? What did he want?"

"That's the sad part, he only did it on a dare as some sort of fraternity stunt. We weren't lovers. We weren't friends. In fact, we'd never even met." Cat looked again at Merrill. "So, you see, it was all fabrication. A world of tinsel and lies. This is real, Carl and Casey are my life."

Opening her fisted hand, she tapped the corner of her eyes. "I earned the crow's-feet and the calluses, and I wouldn't trade them or a single day of this, for the life I had." Reaching out to Merrill, she covered a smaller hand with her own. "Life isn't always what it seems and people aren't as they pretend to be. Sometimes we'll be fooled, and make the wrong choices. Other times, we'll be right. We make the best we can of the first, the errors, accepting no more than our own share of any harm that comes of it."

Her grip eased, softened as did her tone. "For the last, for the times we choose right, for men of honor and courage like Carl and Tynan, we thank God."

The shuffle-thump of Carl's footsteps sounded again in the hall.

Cat listened, and her smile grew tender. "When I was hurt and bitter, he taught me that. Not with words, but with his compassion and his love. Ty would do the same for you, if you let him."

The halting step grew nearer.

"And that, my dear, is the end of my tragic, and not so tragic, story. And the last of my philosophical sermon." As she fell silent and as Merrill watched, lifting her gaze to Carl's as he stood with Casey in the doorway, Cat smiled. Father and son, so much alike, smiled back.

All the tragedy, and all the years faded away. Cat Carlsen was as beautiful as she'd ever been.

Dinner was a lively affair. Neither Casey's handsome but grave countenance nor his silent presence dampened the high spirits. Carl replaced the spicy cider with a pleasing Chianti, and Merrill found herself with yet another drink in her hand.

The spaghetti was wonderful. The recipe for the sauce one of the few good things Cat attributed to her ancestry. Ty surprised everyone, Merrill most of all, by contributing a loaf of her bread for the meal. Having withstood the trip in his back-pack quite well, to her great relief it had been sliced, tasted, judged, and pronounced a fabulous accompaniment for Cat's sauce and Carl's wine.

In an offhand manner that didn't succeed in hiding her pride, Cat announced that the salad of fruit and raisins and nuts was Casey's contribution. His own specialty, put together in the early afternoon before his enforced rest.

"That leaves you, O'Hara," she drawled as she leaned both elbows on the table. "What will be your contribution?"

Pushing back from the table, Ty thought for a moment. "I bring good news. The buffalo are grazing on the unfenced part of my lower meadow. Twenty-two of them, all present and accounted for."

Carl muttered a sound of relief. His dark eyes caught the glitter of the candle smoldering in a wax covered bottle in the center of the table. "I was afraid they were the reason the grizzly took so long to pass through."

Ty had tipped his chair back, now he brought it very carefully back to the floor. "Then you've seen signs of him too."

A grim quirk of Carl's mouth signaled that he had. "He spent some time down by the forks of Triple C Crik. But that was over a month ago and there's been nothing since."

The only tracker in the country better than Carl Carlsen was Tynan O'Hara, though Ty never admitted it. He didn't now as he asked, "What could you tell about it? Male? Female?"

"It was either male, or the largest female in history. From the length of his claw prints and the depression of his tracks, I'd say he was the biggest grizzly I've ever seen. Male or female. I estimate the weight at more than a thousand pounds. From the marks on the trees, it must stand an easy eight feet."

"Big enough to bring down a small horse, or a buffalo." Cat laid a hand on Carl's arm, her tanned fingers pale against his darker skin. "Or a man."

Taking her hand in his, Carl lifted it briefly to his lips. "But not this man."

Rising, Cat busied herself then with the clearing of the table.

When Merrill would have joined her in the kitchen alcove, she waved her away. Sensing that the competent and accomplished woman needed a moment to herself more than she needed help, Merrill stayed at the table.

Carl's worried gaze followed his wife, lingering long on with tender concern before moving away as he returned to the subject of the bear. "He took his time passing through, and I'd put that down to poor hunting ability." He had been toying with the stem of his wineglass as he spoke. He looked up now. "The grizzly lost half of his right front paw."

Ty sat a little straighter. "Recently?"

"Recent enough that he left blood in the snow."

"Are you thinking a trap?" Ty's focus never deviated from Carl.

"Would be my guess." The glass spun one last time, then was still. "He either tore it off fighting the claw of the trap, or chewed it off."

That meant he would be crippled. And mean and hungry. If Ty was concerned before, now he was worried. "When did you first see the sign?"

Carl reeled off a date. "Marked it on the calendar. A week later I tracked him off the range."

"Merrill?"

Merrill had been listening, as she watched Casey covertly, noting a spark of interest in the discussion. "I found tracks in the lower meadow a week before Carl found his. There was no blood in the snow."

Ty blew out a harsh breath. "That means we have two bears trailing through our ranges, or one that got hurt between *Fini Terre* and the Triple C." To Carl he said, "Have you given anyone permission to trap on your land."

"Don't like traps," Carl groused. "Won't allow the abominable things on my land. Legal or otherwise."

"Neither do I." Ty's fist crashed down on the table, rattling the glassware. "Poachers."

"Smells like their kind of rotten stunt. Set an illegal trap, forget it, leave it for an animal to lie in. Suffering, starving, dying a slow death. Or like our bear, making a dangerous cripple of it.'' Grasping the bottle of Chianti by the neck, Carl splashed some into his glass. But as he set it aside, he didn't drink. ''Poachers! Damn them!''

Ty had no more anger to waste on poachers. ''How far did you track him?''

''Miles.'' Carl understood Ty's disquiet and the concern behind the belabored questions. ''Far enough to think he was really moving on and wouldn't be a threat to the stock. My guess is he came out of the park, and was heading back.''

The park, Glacier National Park, was home to the largest number of grizzlies in the lower forty-eight states. ''Going home,'' Ty muttered. ''To stay.''

''Maybe.'' Carl glanced at Cat, who had moved silently to stand at his side. There was little she feared, but the grizzly was among that little. Drawing her hand to his, lacing his fingers briefly over hers, he murmured, ''Sorry, honey. None of us can be sure where a bear might go, or where he might stay.''

''Then you think he might come back.'' Cat's tone was calm, her voice steady, but two lines, like flags of worry, deepened between her eyebrows. Hiding what was quickly becoming terror, she gathered up her husband's plate and returned to the sink.

As Merrill watched, Casey turned his silent gaze from his father to his mother and back again. And then, inexplicably to her. On impact she felt riveted in place by the dormant strength of the boy. If ever she'd thought the lack of speech was an indication of damaged intelligence, this first unfettered look into those keen eyes was enough to shatter any misconception.

Something was bothering the boy. Something he wanted and needed to communicate. Something about the conversation. She'd seen no notepads or pencils around and there had been no mention of any. Apparently he didn't communicate in any way. Yet he understood everything that was said.

Aphasia, with only the speech center involved. Merrill

hadn't seen it before, but she'd heard of it, read of it. The ability to speak remained, but the words would be wrong.

"Will he come back?" Ty addressed Cat's question, trying to reassure her. "I can't think why he would. From what we know, he didn't find this very successful hunting grounds. And he was very likely injured on your land or mine. Added to that, from what Merrill tells me, Shadow gave him quite a chase. With all those odds stacked against him, chances are he won't be drawn back here."

"In any case, he'll be hibernating, or returning to hibernation, soon. If he hasn't already." Carl put in his two cents of encouragement.

Cat turned back from the sink. "Not true hibernation. His body temperature will stay nearly the same. You know that. Which means he can wake up on any mild day. Or, since he can't hunt properly, because he's starving."

"Honey, this isn't the same as before. The bear that mauled me was a rogue." Carl tapped his head. "A little crazy in the head."

"This one may be a lot crazy in the head," she countered. "Since he's crippled."

"That could be," Ty admitted. "But it still isn't likely. We can keep a close watch for a couple more weeks."

"Then if there's no sign of him," Carl amplified the thought. "We can figure he's long gone. Bears aren't exactly the smartest creatures in the world, Cat. And it's not like this is his home territory."

"He came hungry," Ty surmised. "He went away hurt and hungry. He won't be back."

Merrill was still watching Casey. His face was a replica of his father's, beneath a thatch of hair as dark. But his eyes were as green as his mother's, as expressive. As if there were no discussion swirling around her, she concentrated on the boy, willing him to look at her again. Waiting until he did.

There!

Their gazes met, held, amber and gold probed the depths of

darkened green. The raw, desperate need she saw there sent a shiver through her like a jolt of silent lighting.

What? She didn't move, yet a part of her reached out to him, as desperate to understand as he was to be understood.

His struggle drew his mouth into a strained rictus. The softness of youth leached from his face leaving only the hollow eyed gauntness of the strain of a quick and healthy mind trapped in confused silence. His throat worked, a moan he would never allow choked him. His burning stare never turned from Merrill.

"What?" Her whisper was ragged, more resounding than a scream in its own desperation. Sliding her palms over the table, she grasped his wrist. "What is it Casey?"

Conversation stuttered to an abrupt halt. Carl's convulsing hand knocked over his wineglass. The dregs of red wine soaked like blood into his napkin. Cat's shoulders stiffened. With exaggerated care, moving in slow motion, she set down a dish. A towel fluttered to the floor.

She turned to stare.

Then Carl.

Then Ty.

Merrill didn't know, or care. Her thoughts and her attention were riveted on Casey. "There's something you want to say." The flesh beneath her fingers was clammy, the tendons tautly strung. "It's something you need to tell us, isn't it?"

Casey nodded.

Cat took a stumbling step toward her son, halted uncertainly. No one at the table moved. None dared. Each hardly seemed to breathe in the pall of silence as they watched, as they waited.

"Something about the bear," Merrill ventured. Plucking the idea from the recent conversation.

The young, dark head dipped once.

"Yes?"

In response, Casey nodded again. Then, abruptly, shook his head.

"Yes? No?" She faltered, her fingers gripping tighter over the prominent bones of his wrist.

Never looking away from Merrill, Casey repeated the process. A nod, then a turn left and right.

"Yes and no!" Merrill took a wild stab.

Casey smiled. A slow twist of one corner of his mouth. The familiar smile of a Carlsen, easing only a little of the grimness from his features.

"This is about the bear." Merrill frowned in repetitive concentration, fearful she would go in the wrong direction and lose the thread of empathy. "About the bear, but not about the bear."

Casey smiled again.

"But what?" She was stymied, with no idea where to go next.

"Sow." This time his reaction was pure disgust, as he remained completely unaware of the wondering look on the faces of his mother and father and Ty.

"Not a cow." Merrill's mind was ranging, seeking a common ground of cognition. "A dog? A wolf? Shadow?"

Each elicited another negative reaction.

In sudden inspiration, she blurted, "The buffalo?"

A curtly signaled yes. A smile.

"The buffalo, but what about them?" She was pleading now, lost. "Tell me, Casey. Try."

There was nothing. No response. No common ground.

Urgently, under the pain-filled gaze of her dinner companions, Merrill searched her mind, seeking a way or a word that would reestablish her rapport with Casey. Like a teacher calling out the week's spelling test, she rattled words at him.

Dogs. Houses. Fences. Fields. Traps. Hurt. Caves. Sleep. This meadow, or that. *Fini Terre,* or the Triple C. The list went on, striking no spark. And at last, exhausted, she fell silent.

Cat stood as she was, frozen in place, not certain what she felt or understood. Carl's unfathomable gaze never left his son's face. Ty's never turned from Merrill.

The drip of a faucet beat a soft and steady rhythm. The light of the fire spilling over the hearth cast dancing shadows over the floor. Silence spun into feverish tension, keeping them as fiercely as bonds of irons.

Fifteen seconds. Thirty. A minute. No one moved. No one spoke.

No one but Merrill. "I don't know, Casey," she whispered. "You have to help me."

Casey knew what she was asking. A jerk of his head said no.

"Please." Her grasp loosened on his arm. Her touch grew gentle. "Not for me. Not for Ty. Not even for your mom and dad. For you."

In an instant that seemed longer than the minutes that had just passed, Casey didn't respond. Then a low moan sounded in the back of his throat. The young mouth worked. A face that would be even more handsome than either of his parents for its traits of both, crumpled into a fierce mask. His lips moved stiffly, spitting out a garbled sound. A word.

"T...tu...tow."

"Tow?" Merrill deciphered.

Her effort was met with an angry blink.

"Not tow." She tried again, refusing to let him retreat again into silence. "Top?"

Nothing. Not even a blink.

Her mind racing feverishly. She wouldn't let him go. She couldn't. Relentless, she tried again. "Two?"

Fire leapt again into his shadowed gaze. He smiled a tired smile.

"Two! Two bears." Something in his look told her she was wrong. Close, but wrong. "Two buffaloes?"

The smile became a grin, and he was beautiful.

"Twins," Carl whispered suddenly. "I had forgotten. One of the buffalo cows had twins in the summer. When he got out of rehab, I took Casey out to see them."

"Then there should have been twenty-three in the herd." Ty's elation at hearing Casey speak turned grim.

Carl wasn't listening. Neither was Cat as she rushed to take Casey in her arms. Rocking him against her breast, her face pressed into his hair. Her cheeks were dry. Tears clinging to her lashes waited to fall until Carl enfolded both mother and son in his strong embrace.

Turning away, giving the Carlsens a private moment, Merrill sighed wearily. Softly, hopefully, to Ty she murmured, "That there were only twenty-two could be attributed to a number of things."

"Yeah," he agreed gruffly, seeing her fatigue, gauging the emotional cost of the miracle she'd wrought. Touching her cheek with the back of his hand, he skimmed the sculpted curve of it, brushing a wayward tendril away, tucking it behind her ear. A touch that was little comfort for the need in him. The need to hold her, sharing his strength. But it was all he could give. All he could take.

Merrill swayed, leaning into his caress. Her lashes drifted down, color blooming against the pallor of her cheeks like new roses in snow. Sighing again, regretting a moment of weakness, she straightened, moving away.

Color fled again from her face, her hands folded rigidly in her lap. Beneath the practical flannel shirt, her breasts rose in one long hard effort as she struggled for composure. Then another and another, and with each she grew calmer.

"It doesn't have to be the bear," she whispered, catching up the thread of lost thought.

"No." Ty had a little backing up of his own to do. A thought to catch. "Every lost calf doesn't mean a bear. When there are twins, the weaker one often dies."

"It could have fallen behind in their wandering search for grass."

"That's possible."

"There are streams…"

"It might not have been able to cross," Ty finished for her.

"The mother could protect only one from the bear." Ever the realist, Merrill faced a chance as likely.

"Yeah," Ty agreed, this time in visible concern.

"That means he could come back."

"It's possible. There was always the chance of it, Merrill. No matter what happened to the calf."

"Poor little baby."

"You're tired." Ty declared abruptly, scraping back his chair as he spoke. "And the Carlsens have a lot to deal with." He was rising, his hand on her shoulder. "Let's go home, and leave them alone. Carl won't mind if I take the snowplow and return it in the morning."

Ty's voice dragged Carl's attention from his wife and son. Releasing them he circled the table to Merrill. Taking her hand he drew her from her seat. His chiseled face was grave, his dark eyes bright with new hope. He touched her cheek, calloused fingers tender, as if she were more than precious. Bending, he brushed his lips against her forehead.

His searching gaze looked deeply into hers, his hand tightened over her wrists. As if finding what he sought, he nodded swiftly. "Thank you." To Ty he said, "And to you, for bringing her to us."

Carl would say no more.

It was enough.

As quietly as he could Ty guided Merrill to the door. They were shrugging into jackets and donning gloves when Catherine's husky voice called out to Merrill. "You will come again."

"I…" Merrill paused, frightened by the incredible gratitude she saw. It was too much for the little she'd done. With a tiny shake of her head she said, "I'm sorry, I don't think…"

"Please." There was naked need on Cat's face. She was a woman stripped of all pride. She would beg for her son, if she must.

Merrill looked away, unable to bear the burden of hope.

Ty stood at her side. Neither touching her nor speaking. Yet she knew he would be supportive in her decision.

"You must." Cat stood behind her son, her arms lying on his shoulder, her hands linked over his chest. A protective stance, challenging Merrill to deny her.

"I've done nothing, Cat," she said quietly. "Nothing you or Carl, or Ty, or anyone, couldn't have done."

"Dear heaven, Merrill! Don't you think we've tried? Don't you think we've struggled and prayed for this breakthrough. All of us from doctors and therapist to friends and neighbors. Yet none of us has done what you did tonight. None of us could."

"It was simply that the time was right," Merrill argued, discounting her influence.

"The right time, the right person." Cat was tenacious, a mother tiger fighting for her young.

"Cat..."

"Please."

The word was garbled and slurred, but not so much that it wasn't recognizable. Merrill's look dropped at last to Casey. He sat calmly, inert, yet with the same naked hope in eyes so like his mother's.

"Casey," she began, not certain what more she meant to say, or even if there was more.

"Please." The word was no clearer, no less unmistakable. No less a triumph.

Merrill was lost. Even a pathological fear of failing again, was no match for this heart wrenching persuasion. She drew a low, shuddering sigh, and as Ty's fingers linked through hers, she smiled, weakly, and nodded. "I'll be back."

"Promise."

Carl had moved to take his wife back into his arms. He waited for her promise as intently as Cat.

Tynan said nothing. The pressure of his fingers twining through hers never varied as Merrill's grasp grew hard.

The Carlsens were no stranger to tragedy. Now in a chance encounter, she had become their light in the darkness. If they believed she could help, if Casey believed, then perhaps it would be true.

Merrill knew she must try. To Carl, to Cat, to Casey, she vowed quietly, "I promise."

* * *

The Sno-Cat made quick work of the ride through moonlit fields and pastures that were, indeed, the fairyland Carl had promised. Huddled in her corner of the cab, Merrill didn't seem to notice. And loath to disturb her thoughts, Ty didn't call her attention to any of it. As he maneuvered the heavy machine up hills and down inclines, across creeks and through small canyons, he kept his own counsel.

When she was ready, and if she needed him, she would reach out to him. Until then, he would wait.

A lamp in the window welcomed them home, its light glancing off Merrill, marking the fatigue that etched itself deeply on her face. When Ty brought the vehicle to a halt before the door, she made no protest when he touched her cheek commanding, "Wait."

When he crossed in the beam of bright headlights, coming to her side to wrench open the door, she went willingly as he lifted her in his arms, traversing the last of the snowy yard to the house. Welcomed by its warmth, when he held her in his embrace, peeling away her hat and coat, then bent to tug off her boots to toss them aside with her gloves, she was grateful.

There were no cries for propriety and decorum as he loosened her belt and took it away. Nor while her blouse was freed from the waist of her jeans. When he laid her on her bed, tucking the covers close about her, then knelt, looking down at her for a long while, she managed a smile.

A smile. He would be content with that. For now.

Leaning to her, he kissed her cheek, murmuring, "Good night, Santiago. My kind, brave Santiago."

Without another gesture, he left her then, moving with the quiet, familiar ease all his own. With his words echoing in her heart, she lay as she was, listening as he crossed the great room. Then to his fading footsteps as he climbed the stairs to his lair.

Long after the house was still, long after the turmoil of her mind and the race of her heart had quieted, she lifted a palm, clasping it to her cheek, keeping the memory of his kiss.

Seven

"**R**eady?"

Hands on her hips, her feet set in a challenging stance, Merrill glared at Ty. "This isn't necessary, you know. I can ride to the Carlsens' alone."

Ty didn't answer as he continued pulling on his gloves. When he finished, as he reached for his hat, she caught his wrist, holding it.

"I really can, you know," she insisted more in concern than anger. "And you have work of your own to do."

"Nothing that won't keep." Carefully, he peeled her fingers away and lifted his hat from its peg. Setting it at a comfortable angle over his forehead, with a tug at the brim, he stood waiting.

Merrill wasn't ready to give in so easily. "Carl's patrolled the creeks. Criks, he called them," she threw in for good measure. "Along with that he's watched the near meadows for weeks keeping tabs on the buffalo herd. In all that time, he's found no sign of anything to be concerned about. Elk, deer, a moose.'' She ticked off the list succinctly. Then added the clincher. ''Cat has been riding farther and farther afield.''

''Cat is Carl's concern, you're mine.'' The fearless Cat's fear of bear had reached epic proportions after Carl's mauling. Years had done little to assuage it. That she was riding out beyond the safer fringes of their ranch, leaving Casey with Merrill while the two of them had their bi-weekly tête-à-tête, could only mean her confidence the bear was truly gone outweighed alarm.

''Carl swears that if there were even a hint of a bear within forty miles, she wouldn't let him out of her sight, or leave Casey alone at the house.''

Her argument fell on deaf ears. None of what she said mattered to Ty. Arms crossed over his chest, he stubbornly refused to budge an inch from his stand. ''When you're ready, Merrill,'' he said, unperturbed. ''We'll go.''

''I won't let you do this.'' She was every bit as determined and as stubborn. ''You're stretched too thin already. Patrolling the upper meadows, seeing to the stock, spending hours at the Carlsens' waiting for me.'' She looked up at him with an accusing frown. ''I hear you working into the night. Longer each night as the deadline for your book gets closer.''

''The book's fine, right on target. I've always worked longer hours toward the finish. I would if we weren't spending time at the Carlsens'.'' Taking her jacket from the wall, he held it. ''It's your decision. You go, I go. I don't, you don't.'' The jacket hung between them, a line of contention. ''Which is it to be?''

''This is foolish, Tynan.''

He didn't acknowledge her accusation by so much as a flicker of an eyelash. ''Go, or stay? Which is it?''

Flashing an angry look at him, she stepped forward, then turned, slipping into the jacket. But not without tossing one last barb over her shoulder. ''Valentina's vocabulary was woefully inadequate when she said you were stubborn.''

''She was sparing your delicate ears,'' Ty responded mildly, swayed no more successfully by her frustration then her diatribe. "Certainly not my reputation."

"Right." Merrill shrugged the jacket to a more comfortable fit, wondering why worry for Ty made her angry at him. It made no sense at all. Flexing her fingers inside tight gloves, she changed the subject in a tiny capitulation. "Will you take Shadow this time?"

"I promised Casey I would." A silent signal to the wolf brought him leaping from his place by the stove, his tail wagging his body at the exciting prospect of a run. Something akin to a grin curled the fierce mouth as he followed them from the house.

Merrill never asked why Shadow had been denied these outings he loved. Simple deduction and common sense were all that was needed to understand that neither Ty nor Carl wanted to risk losing the bear in a wild chase, as would happen if Shadow ran across its trail.

Swinging into the saddle, holding Tempest to a few kicks and a crow hop or two, Merrill waited until Ty was mounted on Bogart, the big bay he favored. As the saddle creaked from the cold, and with her breath a visible vapor, she voiced her suspicions. "You won't admit it, but you're feeling pretty confident the bear's trek through *Fini Terre* and The Triple C was an isolated incident." Pausing a beat, she pushed her point. "You are, aren't you?"

"What makes you think that?" Following Tempest's lead, Bogart tried a prancing, bowed neck hop or two that brought horse and rider around until they were facing Merrill and Tempest. Satisfied the bay had the little romp out of his system, with a tap at the gelding's neck, Ty calmed him and returned to their conversation. "You've good reason for thinking so, I take it."

"Shadow wouldn't be going if you weren't convinced." Gathering the reins tighter, she backed Tempest away. "Which means you needn't take this time from your busy schedule."

Anticipating that she intended to set the surefooted mare

into a gallop, leaving him behind, Ty bent forward, standing in the stirrups as he caught the end of the reins trailing from her grasp. Bringing Bogart closer, he leaned toward her until they were hip to hip and knee to knee. "There's another reason that I'm going with you, sweetheart."

"Oh yeah?" He'd drawn Bogart even closer. The line of her thigh was pressed against his. No matter that he held the reins, one cluck of her tongue, a shift in the saddle, and Tempest would have moved away, giving her a little space. But she didn't move, and she made no sound as the clean soap and smoke and leather scent of Ty drifted through the sharp, crisp air. "What would that reason be?"

"This." Releasing his hold on her reins, he dropped his Stetson on the pommel of his saddle only a second before tipping hers back. With the same suddenness, giving her no time to think, he crumpled the open edges of her jacket in his grasp drawing her to him. For a moment they were eye-to-eye, his cool gaze probing hers. His mouth was only a blur when his lips crinkled into a rueful smile and he whispered, "Forever this."

The smile was still there when his head dipped. There when his mouth teased over hers sending waves of shivering sensations through her.

Shaken, she jerked away. "What are you doing?"

"I thought that was obvious." His arms closed around her bringing her back to his embrace. "I'm winning an argument."

"Ty!" She would have turned her face away. Two fingers at the tense line of her jaw stopped her.

"Shh." His breath was warm against her cheek as his fingers tunneled into the mass of her hair, holding her, keeping her. He was so close his lashes tangled with hers. His mustache and the seeking lips beneath it grazed her cheek, as he admonished hoarsely, "Don't disturb a man when he's arguing."

As if testing the feel and taste of her, his head tipped down to hers, his lips nibbled, explored, persuaded. Seduced. Promised. She meant not to respond, intent on winning the battle. But intentions were no match for the strength of the wide, hard chest pressed against her breasts. The mesmerizing power of his touch.

She felt herself falling into the spell he wove so well, a pawn in the game he played. In one great effort, reaching into a last reserve of discipline, she shoved him away. In one startled, tremoring moment she was free. But her freedom was short-lived, for in the next, she found herself caught even more tightly, more closely.

"No!" she managed in a great gasp even as the tickle of his mustache at the corner of her mouth sent a hunger she strove to deny to new heights. "No."

His gloved hands on her body were steadfast, unyielding, the latent strength overwhelming. He held her captive as easily as he might have a kitten, or a child, or the woman she was. Yet, dimly, part of her knew that if she fought him, really fought him, he would back away.

She would. She even thought she had, but with the simplest ease his lips found hers again. With the same gentle teasing. The same promise.

The intriguing promise.

Her pulse was pounding, her blood rushing, leaving her dizzy and with her head swimming. Struggling against the clamor of her own body, she would play his game the only way she could, not matching strength for strength, nor obstinance with obstinance. She would meet the madness he created, and the urgency rising like a tide within her, with coolheaded, passive resistance. For one heady increment of time she thought she'd succeeded. That she was passive, that she had resisted. Then, with a flick of his tongue over the curve of her lips, as if her body and mind had waited only for this, her world exploded in a blinding flash of white hot heat.

In a shivering, thrumming red tide, all she'd denied, all she needed for so long, swept any silly imaginings of resisting Tynan O'Hara from her mind.

If her pulse had pounded, now it slowed to a steady drum-

ming, with each shattering, thundering beat shaking every inch
of her. If her blood rushed, now it seethed and churned. As
she trembled with the impact, her muscles went slack, the last
of her tenacity and vigor slipping away. Tension banding her
neck and shoulders eased, as if with the intimate touch cables
of steel were transformed to bands of pliant satin.

Still, she knew she should remember it was a game, only a
game. She should pull away; she should insist that he not hold
her so tightly nor kiss her so cleverly.

She should.

Of course she should, but simmering passion spiraling to
the point of ignition was far more insistent, far stronger.

Far more truthful.

Embers of desire licking at her mind and body, plundered
and mocked even this half rational thought. And as her mouth
opened to his, not in anger or denial, but yearning and urgent,
sleeping passions that slept no more soared beyond mere ignition. Smoldering embers flared in a consuming conflagra-
tion.

Shaken by the sudden reversal, seared by the power of it,
Ty drew away. Only the little needed to look down at her.
The little needed to see what his touch and his kiss had done.
Merrill stared up at him, her breasts rising, pressing against
his chest with each labored breath. Her eyes were huge, the
color gone from them, leaving only the dark, bottomless
depths of bold desire.

Shocked, not by the intensity of her passion, but that it lay
so close to the surface, he would have called on the last shred
of sanity, the last reserve of strength, to move away. He would
have given her space, time to catch her breath. Time to think.
Allowing himself a moment to deal with the avalanche of sensations his kiss had wrought.

Or so he thought. So he intended. Until it was her hands
framing his face and her gaze blazing into his. Until it was
her look scorching with its heat, with aching hunger a rampage
in its depths.

"Damn you," she whispered on a shuddering sigh. The

pressure of her hands slipped to his nape, her finger twining in the shaggy length of his hair, drawing him back to her. Back to her kiss. Her mouth brushed his. Once, twice, lingered, waited. Her nails scored the tender flesh of his neck as her lips teased the clipped edge of his mustache. Her breath quickened, her fingers convulsed in his hair. Her eyes blazed as she turned her head away and back as quickly, yet setting a little space between them.

Her lashes fluttered to her cheeks. A gold tipped fringe veiling her eyes. She was still, silent as stone. Only her hands moved, curling into fists in his hair as she waged one final, paltry battle and lost.

Slowly, her lashes lifted. The storm still raged in her level gaze, even as her taut grasp of his hair became a caress. "Damn you," she whispered as she drew him down to her, harder, closer. This was a game, but not to her. "Damn you, Tynan O'Hara."

"I was. The first moment I saw you." Yanking her to him, closing the little space she'd left, he folded her in his rough embrace. Even if she fought him now, he wouldn't let her go. As his head dipped once more to her, as her mouth opened to him, he muttered, "God help me, I am."

Merrill didn't fight. She was done with fighting.

The last pretense fell away. The last reserve shattered as his mouth devoured hers. Enveloped in the clean, crisp scent of him, with its lingering traces of leather and smoke she gave herself up to the magic he made. Reveling, with no repentance, in the intoxicating taste of the primal male and his primal needs.

There was no gentleness in a gentle companion. No reason in a reasonable man. But reason and gentleness were not what she wanted, nor what she needed.

She forgot time and place and circumstance. She forgot heartaches and tragedy and memories. She forgot everything until Tynan groaned, and leaned his forehead against hers, for once needing her strength.

"We have to go," he murmured as he broke away to draw air into lungs that were starved.

Sensing a change, Tempest sidled a little away, tired of crowding against Bogart, eager for a gallop. Reaching out, Ty settled her down with an absent tug at her mane.

Merrill straightened, taking up the reins in a grasp that was not as steady as she'd like. Dazed, she tried to make sense of what he'd said. "Go?"

"Yes, go. Now." Ty laid his palms on her shoulders, his grip crumpling the fabric of her jacket. "Unless you want me to finish what we started. What I want to do—drag you from the saddle, make love to you—here, now, in the snow."

His body ached with the effort it took not to do exactly as he threatened. He'd only been playing a game, only meant to tease, but the game had gone awry. He hadn't known that even in teasing he would find her seductive and alluring, and irresistible. He hadn't expected that desire and passion smoldered so close to the surface, that it would take only a kiss or a touch to kindle the flame.

Until he looked at her now, he didn't know that at the sight of her disheveled hair and her swollen mouth, he would want to say to hell with the rest of the world. That he would want nothing more than to begin the game that wouldn't be a game all over again.

"Is that what you want, sweetheart." The back of his gloved hand skimmed down her temple, to her mouth. And even with the thin leather between them, touching her was sweet. "Would you make love in the snow?"

"No!" The word spilled from her, even as her body cried yes. The image of Casey waiting by the window, watching for her, eager for her visit, was the only source of her constraint. "You were right, we should go. Casey's waiting." Though he knew, she reminded, "I don't want to disappoint him."

"I know," Ty agreed as needlessly.

"But it would be no, even if he weren't waiting," Merrill flung at him with more than a touch of bravado. "Snow or no snow, making love with you isn't what I want."

"No?" Ty cocked a brow as he studied her face, lingering long on her lips and the all too evident mark of his kiss as he repeated softly, "No?"

"No! N. O." Merrill was suddenly adamant, remembering how the passionate confrontation had come to pass. With a swipe of her arm over her mouth, she snapped, "You picked one hell of a way to win an argument, O'Hara."

Ty looked hard at her for a long while. Then in slow, measured motions, he leaned away from her, took his hat from the pommel and set it firmly on his head. The little ritual complete, he folded his hands before him and shifted in the saddle as he watched her from the shadow of the tilted brim. "Is that what you think I was doing?"

"It's what you set out to do, isn't it?"

"Maybe." Plucking her Stetson from her back, he angled it over her forehead and eased the slide that held it in place to her chin. When she would have cringed away, he ignored it and continued his ministrations—turning up the collar of her jacket, easing a wrinkle from its fabric. Then, grasping the lapels he'd just smoothed, he made her look at him. His own look ranged over her face, tarried at the glittering anger in her eyes, the swollen, just kissed pout of her mouth. His voice was roughened, his tone mild, when he said, softly, "Then again, maybe not."

"Tynan…"

"Shh." A leather clad finger slanted over her lips, stopping any comment. "Careful, you aren't out of the woods yet, honey."

Pushing his hand away, her chin jutted at a challenging angle, hoping with all her might that he wouldn't suspect how close she'd come to the edge. "Then what do we do?" In a lazy, mocking drawl, she added, "What next, O'Hara, honey?"

"We ride." With a whistle to Shadow, who had gone to investigate a snowdrift, he gripped the reins, pulling them up short. Bogart quivered at the signal, needing only the tap of a spur to fly.

"We."

"Yes, we." He grinned at her. "I won the argument, remember."

Her expression was all innocence, and all a lie. "Did you?"

"Maybe." In a move she didn't anticipate, he caught her chin in the curl of his palm. His slanting kiss was quick and sweet, and over even as it began. The grin was still in place, but a little ragged at the edge. There was no laughter in his eyes. "Then again, maybe not."

With a touch at the brim of his Stetson in the gallant western salute, he raked his spurs over Bogart's flank. It was the invitation the well-trained cow horse had awaited. The gelding didn't need another. Snow flew in his wake as broad hooves tracked over virgin snow.

Tempest reared and lunged and fought the tight hold of her reins. Sawing on them, backing the mare away, Merrill was tempted not to follow.

But Casey waited.

And what would be the point? Of what worth was a skirmish won, after the battle was lost?

"All right, girl." Merrill leaned down to stroke the flowing mane. "Let's show them how it's done."

She rode then as Ty rode, hard, fast, recklessly. With Shadow tracking by her side, and desire a quiet companion, awaiting another day.

"Hello."

Casey hailed them from the porch of the ranch house when they were barely in sight. As Tempest and Bogart slipped and slid down the last hill, he was descending the steps, with a confidence that grew each day. By the time they halted the horses at the weathered hitching post, he was waiting there, a beaming smile nearly splitting his face in half.

"Well, look at you," Merrill declared as she swung from the saddle and turned to embrace him. With a kiss on his cheek, she held him at arm's length. "I leave you for half a week and look what you do. You look like you just rode the tornado deck of a bucking bronc and stayed on. And to top it all, I would swear you've grown an inch.''

Casey lifted his shoulders as a blush added to the color the sharp air had drawn to his face. ''And you,'' he tapped her chin. ''Practicing cowboy lingo.''

The words were halting, the phrase punctuated with sporadic pauses, but the meaning was clear.

''I've been reading,'' Merrill admitted.

Casey grinned. ''Read more.''

''Oh?'' Merrill was all innocence. ''Did I get something wrong?''

The boy rolled his eyes at Ty.

Ty grinned back, as aware of the word game Merrill played as Casey. ''We know that in proper cowboy slang, it's the hurricane deck of a bucking bronc. But be patient with her, boy.'' He ruffled the dark hair that barely showed shaggy signs of the trauma Casey had suffered. ''She's a tenderfoot and a gal to boot.''

''Pretty.''

''Well now,'' Ty crossed his arms over his chest and rubbed his chin as he pretended to consider. His considering took a long, thorough time. ''There's no denying that. Her eyes are pretty. They can be a little angry now and again, but that only makes them prettier. And her hair reminds me of your mom's, and it's almost as gorgeous. Then there's her chin. A little stubborn, wouldn't you say? Can't deny that her nose fits right nicely where it sits.''

Casey laughed, once a rare sound, but not since Merrill had come into his life.

Tynan hadn't finished his questionable tabulation of her attributes. ''But do you know what I like best about little Short Bear, Casey?''

Still grinning, Casey shook his head.

''Her mouth,'' Tynan said softly. ''What I like best is her mouth. Makes a man's own mouth water for a taste of it.''

Merrill had listened to enough. Stepping in front of Casey, giving her back to Ty, she touched his face, feeling the cold.

"What have you been doing that has you so mischievous? And why were you waiting here in the cold?"

"Something." His grin faded. He took her hand in his. "Something to show."

Without ceremony he tugged her toward the house. The steps had been cleared, the porch was dry, and Casey moved across it with confident ease. It was then that Merrill realized, it wasn't that he had grown, but that he stood straighter, taller. There was renewed strength in his body, and every shred of hesitance had fallen before the vigor of confidence.

"Casey." She caught at their joined hands with her free hand, slowing him at the door. "What is it? What has excited you so?"

"See." He shook his head, not satisfied with the single word. His eyes closed tightly, his teeth bit at his lip as he searched for the proper word, the proper order. "You shall see."

He beamed at Merrill, not caring that the phrase was stilted, the words not so crisp. What mattered was that he had put together a sentence in perfect sequence.

"What will I see?" Merrill gripped long, slender fingers proudly. "Something special?"

"Hope."

"A surprise? Inside?" Ty put in. Without waiting for Casey's affirmation, he reached past them to push open the door. "Then what are we waiting for?"

For all his eagerness, Casey hesitated, looking about, a frown beginning on his face. "Shadow?"

"I didn't forget, Casey." Tipping his Stetson from his head, and shaking snow fallen from a low hanging limb from the shoulders of his jacket, he crumpled the battered brim in his hard grasp. "He found a scent he couldn't resist, but he'll be along in a minute."

"Good. Shadow's fun."

The same effort was required to find the right words, formulate the sensible sentence, but at least Casey never stopped trying. But for Ty, anything, any effort at all was better than the silent, defeated existence the boy had lived before Merrill. "You won't be so glad if he's disturbed a skunk's cold weather den," he warned. "You remember what happened last year?"

Casey grinned and pinched his nose. A spontaneous gesture and right on target. "Peeyew."

"Exactly," Ty concurred. "In any case, and any condition, Shadow will be along in a bit. Now," he herded them through the door. "What is this great surprise you have for Merrill?"

The house was quiet. With no set timetable for their arrival, Cat and Carl had evidently gone about their chores, leaving Casey to play welcoming committee and host. Another indicator for Cat's renewed confidence in his safety.

With an eager assurance, not giving them time to shed their coats, or brush the snow from their boots, the wounded young man led them to a worktable. There were wood shavings and tool scattered over it. And in the center of the table stood what was obviously a figure covered with a rough cloth.

With a sweep of his arm, Casey indicated that they should sit. With palpable excitement he waited until they were settled and waiting. "Ready?"

With a lancing fear of what hacked and clumsy creation she might see, Merrill looked desperately at Ty. Instinctively he reached out to her, covering the hand that clutched the arm of her chair with his.

"We're ready." His voice was deep and calm and steady, the clasp of his hand strong and tight. "Show us what you've done."

For a moment Casey's exuberance faltered. Old doubts came back to haunt him. With the edge of the cloth only inches beneath his hovering fingers he hesitated.

"It's all right, Casey." Ty spoke again, this time his calm was infectious. "There's nothing you can't show us."

Casey tried to smile. But the joy that had him waiting and watching for them had become doubt.

"Please." Merrill encouraged, joining forces with Ty.

The boy nodded, too filled with conflicting emotions to

struggle for the right word. The cloth moved in only fractions of an inch at first. Then with an impatience to have done with it, he snatched it away.

"My God." Ty's startled prayer rang through the huge room and echoed amid the rafters of the tall ceiling.

And then there was silence.

Casey stood, the cloth clutched against his chest, his riveted stare turning from Merrill to Ty and back again.

"Casey." His name was a strangled sound emitted from a throat that threatened to close. If Merrill's hand had been larger, stronger, the arm of her chair would have broken. Her startled eyes had no time for anything but the figure gracing the center of the shabby worktable. A figure repeated again in a small, delicate watercolor.

"I've never..." her voice faltered, fading away. Swallowing the threat of tears, she tried again, and failed. "I've never seen anything so...so..."

"Beautiful," Ty finished for her. "Nor have I, Casey."

"Merrill," the young artist said simply.

"Yes." Ty hadn't needed to be told. No one in the world who knew Merrill would need it. In both painting and carving, the small figure was perfect down to the last detail. Down to the moccasins she wore most days when she rode. The moccasins she wore today.

In both she wore jeans, an old favorite shirt. A knife was belted at her waist, and a Stetson tipped over her forehead. A saddle was slung over her shoulder, and Shadow lay at her feet. And every part of it, every nuance, stayed true, perfect to the last detail.

"When?" Merrill asked, her voice still filled with wonder. "How?"

"He began the day after you were here for the first time." Carl stood in the door, with Cat a step behind. "We'd tried for weeks to get him to take up his paintbrush and carving tools. We thought it would set him on the path to recovery." He turned to Merrill, addressing her alone. "Until you, he had no interest.

"He worked in secret in his room." A fond look passed between father and son. "When we thought he was sleeping, he'd found better things to do with his afternoons."

Casey nodded and touched the figure of wood.

Carl and Cat advanced into the room. The door swung shut behind them. "The carving was most difficult. At first it was no more than a chunk of wood. Not even the sort he usually worked with. Just something that caught his fancy."

"It lay there on his bedside table, untouched for weeks." Stripping off her gloves, Cat patted Casey's cheek. "Maybe, subconsciously, he was looking for a subject. Something the wood would become. Maybe he simply wasn't ready."

"Then Merrill came along." Ty's fingers laced through hers as he smiled at her.

"He wanted to give her something." Carl looked from the replica of Merrill to Merrill herself. "Something of himself."

"Me!" Merrill jerked forward in her chair, her back straight, her expression filled with surprise. She turned from Casey, then to Ty as if trying to understand. "I couldn't! It's too important."

"You," Casey insisted. "Yours."

"No," Merrill shook her head. "I can't. It's far too valuable, and must mean far too much to all of you to part with it."

"You." Casey pushed the small carving closer to her. "Yours."

"The carving may be of me," she said in agitation. "And I'm flattered that I was its inspiration. But can't you see that I can't take it."

The look of hurt that crossed his face, brought a rush of tears to her eyes. Before she could say more, it was Ty who spoke instead.

"She'll accept it, Casey, when she understands." Taking her hand back in his, to Merrill he said, "The first day we came here, the first time you saw Casey's paintings and carvings and realized he had done mine, I told you something about them. Do you remember?"

Carl and Cat flanked their son. They understood as well as Ty what it meant to Casey for Merrill to have this carving. Especially this carving. Neither would try to persuade her, for in persuasion some of the joy goes out of giving. So they waited and watched, and hoped Ty could make her understand as well.

"I remember." She could never forget. "You told me that Casey always said when the time came, it would be commissioned work that would carry a price tag."

Rising from her chair, Merrill wandered the room. Touching this figure or that. A pony, the eagles, a silly pine marten curled around the cone of a western larch. A whimsical watercolor of a fawn curiously investigating a stalk of white, blooming beargrass. By the figure of a wolf pup chewing on a bridle, she paused.

Ty had watched her ramble. Because he was beginning to understand Merrill better than anyone in the world, he knew that she was drinking in the wonders such a diverse talent could create. Realizing that yes, she played a part in preserving it.

"And," he prodded her from her reverie.

"And these come from his heart." She was moving again, stopping only when she came to the worktable. "This," she traced the line of the sculpture with a fingertip. "This came from his heart, and his heart isn't for sale."

To Casey she said, "I'm flattered and I'm pleased that such an astounding talent chose me as subject for his return to both painting and carving. I'll be more than proud to have it as my own."

The room broke into jubilant celebration, with Casey blushing even more furiously when Merrill rose on tiptoe to whisper a private thanks, sealed with a kiss.

"Well now," Carl drawled. "That's the first time we've had to twist someone's arm to get them to take one of Casey's figures."

"It will be the last." Merrill was laughing in delight. "I predict a great future for Casey Carlsen."

"If it weren't so early, I'd break out some champagne," Cat declared from her place by her son. "Stay for dinner. Take potluck with us and we'll crack the best bottle then."

"The Sno-Cat's yours for the taking, if you'll stay." This from Carl, who smiled as Merrill had never seen him smile.

This, she thought, was how he must have smiled at Cat the day she fell in love with him.

"Merrill?"

Drawing herself from her speculations, she found Ty standing at her side. "I'm sorry. What did you say?"

"Would you like to stay?"

It took her only long enough to say the words. "Yes. I'd like that."

Ty smiled and called over his shoulder. "Casey, there's an inscription of the carving, isn't there?"

For once no one minded that Casey didn't bother with struggling for the right word and nodded instead.

"I think you'll find it on the bottom, Merrill," Ty said. "If Casey runs true to habit."

Taking up the small figure in both her hands, holding it as if a breath or a wrong move would break it, Merrill read the scrawled inscription aloud. "My eternal gratitude to…" Stopping she looked to Ty, and then to Casey before continuing. "To Short Bear."

She had been loved and respected unconditionally only once before. Now, with the use of the silly name Matt Danvers had given her, she knew she was again.

"Thank you." She could manage no more as she set the figure back in its place. No more was needed.

"Bear!" Carl exclaimed smoothing over a charged moment. "I have news. The park service ran a rogue bear to ground and moved him to a distant and isolated region of the park. A big male, with a wounded paw."

"This distant and isolated region." Cat laid a protective hand on Carl's shoulder, never forgetting how close she'd come to losing him to just such a bear. "It's too far for him to ever come back?"

Carl grinned and turned his head to kiss a chapped knuckle. "Way too far. Subject resolved and closed."

Cat was on the porch, her shoulder leaning against a post, her arms crossed over her breasts, when Merrill went in search of her.

"How is he?" She asked without turning, expressing a mother's eternal concern. "Carl and I see him every day, and we watch him so closely, sometimes I think we miss the small progresses."

"He's sleeping now, with Shadow lying at the foot of his bead. He's fine, and he's going to be fine, Cat. No, better than fine. Complete recovery will take time, but not as long as it once was."

Crossing her arms closer, tugging at the collar of her jacket, Cat asked, "Do you ever think that the things that happen to us were meant to be?"

"Some." Merrill leaned on a balustrade. In the corral by the barn, Ty helped Carl change a sagging rail. "I'm not a fatalist. I can't believe we're completely at the mercy of fate."

"No, but look at us. The five of us. Each with his or her own problem. Each with a solution for the other. Carl for me. Ty for you." She folded the collar closer. "He was a lot like you when he came to Montana. An idealist whose ideals had grown tarnished. He found a new perspective here, but even so, he was growing more and more insular, until you came along."

She turned to face Merrill for the first time. "There's a lot unresolved between you, but you've been good for each other."

"Tynan told you about Tall Bear?"

"He thought it would help us understand your empathy with Casey."

"You know the rest? My family, their disappointment in me. The children."

"The children you think you should have saved." There was sympathy in Cat's windburned face. "Maybe you should have, and maybe you would have, if their lives had been in your hands alone.''

"But people aren't always what they pretend to be.'' Merrill was quoting Cat from another time. "Sometimes we're fooled and make the wrong choices. Other times we're right. So, we make the best we can of our errors, accepting no more than our share of the blame for the harm that comes of it.''

"A creed we all must live by, if we are to survive.''

"I'm learning. I'll never forget the past, but everyday I come closer to believing as you do.''

"As all of us have come to believe. Especially Ty.''

Merrill was quiet for a while. The rail was repaired, Ty and Carl were coming in for dinner.

"Why did Casey name the carving Short Bear?''

"He liked the name. He decided it fit you.''

"Why?''

"Because you're tiny.'' Cat pushed away from the post, waiting for Carl as he climbed the stairs. "And as his father's people often believe, Casey believes you have the courage, the strength, and the magic of the bear.''

Her comment was almost lost in the stamp and thud of heavy boots. Perhaps it was fate that had Ty smiling down at her saying softly, "Hi, Short Bear. Did you miss me?''

As she slipped her arm through his, Merrill knew that she had. And when the time came for her to leave Montana, she knew that Tynan O'Hara, the man who had made it his journey's end, would live in her heart forever.

Eight

"Easy, girl." Merrill drew a currycomb through Tempest's rippling mane, never missing a crooning note. As she stroked and patted, whiskered lips nibbled at her shoulder. Laughing, she pushed the massive head away. "You like that, do you?"

Bending, she scratched at Shadow's ears as he curled around her knees wanting his share of affection. Never to be upstaged, Tempest nudged at Merrill's elbow and crowded against her, almost pitching her over. "Don't be jealous, madam, there's enough love to go around."

As she regained her balance, wrapping her arms around the mare's bowed neck she leaned her head against the gleaming mane. "So, do you think you'll miss me when I'm gone?"

"Thinking of leaving us so soon, Short Bear?"

Startled, Merrill whirled to face him. "Ty! I didn't hear you come in."

Chuckling to himself, Ty pushed away from a supporting post where he'd paused to watch the playful interaction between what must be the strangest coterie of friends west of the rising sun. They made a pretty picture there in the stall, with a shaft of light flowing through the window catching motes of dust, filling their small space with a golden haze that sifted around them like stardust.

"You were a trifle busy." What he left unsaid was that he'd come quietly into the barn, hoping for this moment. He never tired of watching her with them. A woman who weighed far less than either wolf or horse, controlling both with a word and a loving pat. That Shadow was a sucker for a gentle touch had long been established. But never like this. Tempest, on the other hand, was another matter. "You've spoiled them, you know."

Folding his arms over the stall portal, he reached out to scratch Tempest while she snuffled curiously at the pocket of his jacket. Rewarding the mare's persistent search with a cube of sugar, he pushed her firmly away. "You've made a pet of this silly creature. When the ranch hands and guides return in Spring, they won't recognize her."

He was so close. Even with the wooden barrier between them, having him so near quickened the beat of Merrill's heart. The cool, crisp fragrance of evergreen and fresh air clung to him, blending with his own familiar scent, surrounded her with pleasant memories. He moved like a phantom in her thoughts, but as she watched him from the corridor, there was substance and seductive reality in the breadth of his shoulders and the corded leanness of his body. And though his face was hidden by the slanting eclipse of the brim of his Stetson, she knew there would be mischief in the curl of his lips, and laughter in his eyes.

"Perhaps I have petted her a bit." Out of habit she complied as Tempest presented her forelock to be scratched. "Do you mind?"

"Why should I?" Catching a curl that always seemed to defy the band at her nape, he twirled it around his finger, discovering that even in dusky half light its many hues were lustrous and golden. A ribbon of silk, he thought, captured in a hand more accustomed to the harsh pull of a rope, or the saw of a rein. "You've spoiled all of us."

"All?" As he wound her hair around his hand, and as his knuckles brushed the sensitive flesh beneath her jaw, Tempest and Shadow were forgotten. "Even you?"

"Especially me." A gentle tug brought her closer. "Most especially me."

"How so? When I've ruined your winter solitude?" She'd been right, there was laughter in his eyes. And something more. Something still and quiet that made her voice grow whispery and vague. "I've filled your house with my clutter, rummaged in your private possessions, interrupted your writing. And, on principle, been a nuisance."

"On whose principle?" He was speaking nonsense. Simply uttering words that had nothing to do with what he was thinking, what he was feeling, or wanted to say.

"Mine." The word was a husky murmur. "Yours," she added quietly as she swayed toward him, mesmerized by him, going willingly wherever he might lead.

"You haven't been a nuisance, you aren't given to clutter, nothing I have is private from you. And my writing can only be the better for such a lovely interruption."

The barn was chilly, kept just warm enough that the livestock wouldn't suffer the cold. But the last brought its own flush of warmth. A slow trembling tension closed her throat and turned the pounding of her heart to thunder. "A pretty compliment."

"No." The width of the door was a chasm. Her mouth, only inches from his, was much too far away. "Truth, not praise." He felt the sudden rush of her breath against his cheek, and almost lost the thread of his chatter. "There will be other winters, time enough for solitude."

But would he want them? he wondered. Could he bear the long, lonely days? Would the solitude he'd cherished be no more than emptiness now that she'd shared a part of his world?

Long. Empty. Lonely. The words echoed in his mind.

Empty.

Lonely.

"Merrill." There was sudden disquiet in him. Perhaps for the life he'd lived. Perhaps for his life as it would be. But as his lips brushed over hers at last, while his Stetson tumbled to the floor and he bent to drink deeply of the passion she brought to him, none of it mattered. Neither yesterday, nor tomorrow. There was only today, only this. Only Merrill.

Touching her, letting his fingers glide over her hair, soothed him. Even as the fires of desire blazed steadily and the yearning grew. He wanted more than a kiss. More than a touch. He'd wanted her at the homestead, on the floor, with the fire burning, and moonlight drifting through the windows. He'd wanted her on the bluff, buffalo grazing at their feet, the threat of a rogue grizzly in the air. He'd wanted her in the snow, meeting challenge with challenge, strength for strength, with a hunger that wouldn't have felt the cold.

He wanted her now and here. In the barn, with straw as their bed, and only honesty between them. With her dusky skin and her rippling hair as golden as the haze. Stardust, yet not.

"Sundust," he muttered, coining a new word as he drew away. The perfect word.

As if he'd been given the cue he'd been waiting for, Shadow rose from the corner of the stall where he'd lain quietly. His tail moved tentatively. Responding to his mood, Tempest tossed her mane and whickered as she nudged at Merrill's shoulder.

A reminder for Merrill, for all she'd forgotten. All his touch and his kiss swept from her mind.

When she would have turned to the horse, he stopped her with a fleeting touch. "You never answered my question."

She heard, but his words seemed to come from far away. Her head turned from side to side, her scattered wits not tracking with the direction he'd taken.

She was heavy eyed and languid, as he'd imagined she would be when he made love to her. A look that was almost his undoing. Only the scrub of a day old beard flushing her cheeks, reminded there were better times and better places. With a finger at her chin, simply because he wanted this small contact, he reminded, "I asked if you were thinking of leaving us so soon?"

It took her a while to find her voice, and then it was rough and unsteady. "Only long enough for a ride to the Carlsens', then another with Casey. He's ranging farther and farther afield, and I promised we would ride as far as the homestead for a picnic. I didn't think you would object."

She'd been riding back and forth between the ranches alone for more than a week. But a niggling worry settled in the back of Tynan's mind and never left. "You'll be careful?"

"I would guard Casey with my life."

Ty had never doubted that. Should something untoward happen, it was the cost to this small, brave woman that he feared. "You'll keep the rifle loaded and close at hand?"

"Always."

Ty relaxed, but only by a little. She would be safe again at *Fini Terre*, before he was at ease. Yet no one knew better than he that he couldn't let his fear for her, when there seemed to be little to fear, keep her prisoner. Careful to keep concern from his tone, he asked, "Then, why should I mind? In any case, I wouldn't want Casey to be disappointed. What you've done for him is a miracle."

"If I could work miracles, I would have him well and sound now, Ty. Not in the future."

"Call it what you like, Short Bear. To Carl and Cat and to me, Casey is a miracle in progress. Thanks to you."

Merrill chose not to argue, settling it succinctly. "Then it remains a matter of opinion."

Ty agreed. "I suppose it does."

The cant of the sun was changing. The stable had darkened as it rose higher, its light falling on rooftops instead of windows. "That's it then?" she didn't move away from the door, but slipped her hands into the pockets of her jeans to conceal their trembling. "Have I answered all your questions?"

"Have I?" he countered.

His gaze was dark and intense in a craggy, weathered face. His hair had grown long in the weeks since she'd become his unwanted guest. It tumbled over his forehead in loose curls even the Stetson couldn't subdue. Barely resisting the urge to smooth them back, she looked at him in question.

"You asked if you would be missed when you're gone." His thumb traced the curve of her lower lip, a hedonistic reminder of his kiss. "Have I answered for myself?"

Catching his hand in hers, Merrill turned her mouth into his palm. The kiss she left there was her answer.

Ty nodded and stepped away. "I'll leave you to get ready. You've a long ride today."

"Not so long. I won't tire Casey too much."

"It isn't Casey I worry about."

Merrill caught back a trembling breath. "I know."

"You know, too, don't you, that one day there won't be anything standing between us. No doubts nor regrets for past sins. No late night rides, no snow. No kind promises to Casey." He tapped the half door of the stall. "Not one barrier of any kind."

"I know." Her admission was just more than a whisper. "I've known for a long time."

Ty stared at her for a great while. The darkness of his gaze reaching into her, seeing all she hadn't the courage to say. "Just so you understand."

"I understand," she said in a tone as hushed. "I have from the first."

In an abrupt move, Ty bent to pluck his hat from the floor. Crushing it in his hand, he looked at her again. "Take care, Short Bear," he murmured at last. "If not for yourself, then for me."

She had no reply. She hadn't the words for what was in her heart. As he left the barn in his usual long and easy step, she watched him, remembering he had called her by the name given her by her beloved Tall Bear. Not just once, not twice, but three times, Ty had called her Short Bear. A silly name, some would think. But for Merrill, it was a name synonymous with unconditional respect and unquestioning love.

For reasons of his own, Casey had given the name to the carving he'd made of her. He thought it fit, Cat had said. Because, though she was small in stature, she possessed the courage and strength of the bear.

Merrill understood without being told that it wasn't physical strength and courage that Casey saw. But strength of heart and mind and soul, the courage of convictions and the will to do what one must.

She'd been that woman once. Perhaps she was almost that woman again.

"Not yet," she said only to herself. "But soon."

To Ty's retreating back, she promised, "Then the last barrier will be gone."

She watched him step through the door and disappear into the morning before she turned to saddle Tempest.

Their ride was pleasant and meandering, with Casey leading the way through a series of shortcuts Merrill was discovering these Montanans knew and used out of necessity. "Forty miles," she muttered, recalling the distance Ty had quoted by road from *Fini Terre* to The Triple C, the nearest ranch. "But not as the crow flies," she added in what was also one of Carl's favorite axioms.

One she easily understood as Casey's horse skirted patches of snow, then threaded through a passage so confining a pregnant mare would have difficulty traversing it. While she followed where he led, they rode ever deeper and farther where no vehicle could go. The sheer face of the trail towered far above them blocking the sun. Yet as the temperature dropped it was never unpleasant. Even here in a place that rarely felt the heat of its rays, water ran in rivulets down walls of stone, and dripped in icy puddles along the trail in a rare thaw.

In the midst of this doldrumlike siege of peculiarly mild temperatures, Cat had jokingly laid the cause on Merrill's presence, declaring she had enchanted all of Montana, even its weather. Carl had only grinned and shook his head, predicting Mother Nature was only saving up for a helluva Thanksgiving or Christmas present.

"Okay, Charley, we're almost through." Urging his suddenly balking mount through a narrowing turn with a firm hand, Casey laughed. "The only horse in the world with claustrophobia, and he's mine."

Tempest picked up some of the big sorrel's jittery mindset, but settled reasonably with a squeeze of Merrill's knees. "Have you ever thought he might just be getting back at you for his name."

"Charley Horse is a perfectly good name."

"Sure it is."

"Lord knows, he's given me enough of them," the boy declared in his own defense.

"Can't say that I blame him." Merrill was smiling at the broad, straight back as she followed. She was just beginning to see Casey as he'd been before the accident. The wicked sense of humor, the quick wit. Every day he came closer to being that unique person again. More and more, as just now, his sentences fell in perfect order with less and less hesitant effort. Words like claustrophobia came quicker, tripped off his tongue naturally. One could only think that in all the long months he would say nothing, the deep-seated injury healed, his synapses busily repairing themselves. So much so, that when he ventured to speak at last, his recovery was amazing, with phenomenal speed.

"Just living up to his name, you think?" Casey surmised over his shoulder as the path grew tighter and the horse more nervous.

"Could be."

"Then I should have called him Aladdin."

"For a ride like a flying carpet?"

"Exactly."

The last crowding turn opened into a meadow still covered with thick tatters of snow. The land rolled gently beneath an unclouded sky. Nothing could have been more open or unconfining, but Charley was still agitated, fighting the reins and rolling his eyes.

"Maybe I should just call him Glue." Casey was only half teasing this time as the gelding's antic grew contagious sending Tempest into a little hopping dance. "Remind me to ride another horse when we come back in the Spring. Or maybe we should just climb over like Shadow has. A rock climb or the trail, however we come, you're in for a treat. The whole field will be carpeted with wild flowers. In fact, mom calls this Wildflower Canyon."

"I'd like to see that, but I won't be here in..."

Merrill's regret was never finished and would never be.

With a terrified scream, Charley reared and pawed, nearly tearing Casey's arms from their sockets. Mad with panic, the sorrel wheeled and squealed in an insane frenzy, bumping Tempest and triggering a like mood in her.

Watching in horror, even as she struggled to keep her own seat, Merrill cried out as a mighty lunge sent Casey tumbling head over boot heels into a bank of snow. And towering over him stood a mountain of glaring, roaring, silver tipped menace.

Grizzly!

With only half of a right front paw.

The terrifying recognition registered in unconscious vignettes as Tempest gave one last mighty buck and Merrill landed flat on her back on a muddy scrap of bare, soaked earth. Rolling, turning, scrabbling to all fours while sucking oxygen into lungs sealed by the impact of her fall, she saw that the snarling, quivering creature, as confused and startled as she, seemed to be more aware of the horses.

"Stay down, Casey. Don't move," she called in the icy calm settling over her. Either the boy heard and obeyed with a will of iron, or he was unconscious. Whatever the case, it wouldn't be long before the bear would recognize there was easier, closer prey for the taking.

A quick look revealed a small cul-de-sac bordered by walls as stark and barren as the passage in. The thrashing, milling horses had gathered against a far wall, with the grizzly blocking both the way in and the way out.

"My rifle." She was muttering now to herself, and hardly aware that she spoke aloud in the chaotic din of screams and snarls. "Hold tight, Casey. Stay as you are."

The last was a prayer as she rose to her feet. The bear was between Merrill and the horses. Between her and the rifle. She hadn't a doubt he would charge when she moved. But she had no other choice.

"Stay Casey. Dear God, please stay." The litany had become a prayer as she edged along the canyon wall. A little more to the right and in a mad dash, maybe she could skirt a copse of fallen stone, keeping it as shield from this maddened creature.

"Maybe," she muttered and cursed softly as a stone dislodged under her moccasined foot and rolled with a deafening clatter down a small incline. "Maybe not."

The bear had turned toward her, its nose lifted to test the air. She saw then that the giant omnivore was thin to the point of starvation, and likely awake and crazed by the pain of it. Casey chose that time to turn and flail in the snow, giving an already derange beast one more target for his ire.

"No!" Merrill cried and began to run. For one turbulent second the grizzly's great head swung toward her. And Casey moved again, coming to a crouch. "No," she screamed again, knowing the boy had never been unconscious and was deliberately drawing the bear to him. As the broad snout bent to sniff, realizing that here there was truly easier prey, Merrill ran with tears on her face, sickness lurching in her throat, denial on her tongue. "No."

The last was a whisper, lost in a whirling furor as a savage, snarling Shadow launched like a black missile from a stone ledge. Merrill heard the cries, and Shadow's yelp of pain. The swat of a huge paw sent the wolf flying as if he were no more than an irritating insect. She heard the frenzied howl as Shadow scrambled again to the fray, but she didn't slacken her pace, nor turn from her goal.

Wild with terror, Tempest reared and dodged, but a lucky catch and a vicious yank at the reins drew her down. Without pause, Merrill stripped the rifle from its case, screaming as she spun about. "Get down, Casey."

Trusting the coolheaded boy would obey and not wasting the time to aim, as she called on her training with The Black Watch, she fired from the hip, advancing with each shot. With a last, mighty slash at Shadow, the grizzly turned to this newest front of attack. Merrill fired and advanced. The maddened creature kept coming. The rank scent of bear and blood and her own fear filling her lungs, she fired. The grizzly faltered, stumbled. She fired again, and again. The maimed, starving beast fell at her feet.

With only the sound of her fierce, laboring breath in her ears, she prodded the brute once with the barrel of her rifle. With a low moan and the weak flailing of a mutilated paw, the last echo of a life ended.

Then the canyon was quiet.

"Ouch!" Dropping the hoof he was inspecting, and scrubbing his hand over his backside, Tynan straightened to face Bogart. "Why did you do that?" The horse didn't react by so much as a flicker of an eyelash, but he would have sworn he saw laughter in the dark, glittering eyes. "How would you like it if I bit you every time I was out of sorts?"

The harangue was not so unusual, for like his brothers and his sister Valentina, Tynan talked to animals. And any who saw and heard would swear the creatures understood.

"That's what it is, isn't it? You're out of sorts because Tempest and Shadow had a day out and you didn't. You miss them, don't you? Well, to tell you the truth, so do I.

"But it shouldn't be too long now." Moving to the other side, he lifted another hoof, this time keeping any likely targets well out of reach. Satisfied the slight limp Bogart had developed was only a stone bruise and temporary, he set the hoof down. Glancing toward the horizon and the hill marked by the well worn trail leading to The Triple C, he smiled. "In fact, it won't be long at all. Shadow isn't with them, but I see the ladies. I wonder what kept them so long? Must have been some handsome scalawag who…''

His bantering mood vanished. Shielding his eyes from the fiery reflection of the first of sunset falling over random drifts of snow, he stared hard. ''What the devil? She's walking. Why would she be…''

Blood drained from his face. His heart was leaden, and his tongue lay like burned wood against his lips. ''No!'' The words were harsh and fearful. A prayer and a plea. ''Dear God, no!''

Clutching at a palmful of mane, in a leap he swung fiercely to the wide, bare back of the gelding. Sensing the change and the urgency in his master, no other signal was needed. The instant Tynan's weight settled securely, Bogart launched himself across the corral, taking the fence as if it weren't there. The path they took should have been treacherous now, with the runoff of melting snow just beginning to refreeze as the day lost the warmth of the sun.

Tynan wasn't concerned about treacherous paths, for if Tempest was the most surefooted horse on ice and snow, Bogart was second. But first or second, third, or last, even then it wouldn't have mattered. For all that concerned and frightened him was Merrill, why she was afoot, and why, in the rapidly plummeting temperature, she wore only jeans and a shirt.

Something was wrong. He sensed it, felt it, knew it, as he rode like a demon to her.

Merrill plodded, her shoulders drooping in the aftermath of crushing fatigue. Head down, she watched her feet, putting one in front of the other, then repeating the pattern all over again. She didn't feel the cold, she didn't smell the blood. With one hand clinging to Tempest's reins like a lifeline and the other lying on the precious burden the mare carried, she simply took each step. And each step brought her one step closer to Tynan.

"Merrill?"

Her name came from far away, barely penetrating her single-minded determination. Certain she was only dreaming, she took one more step.

"Merrill!"

Then Tynan's arms were around her, his palm cupping her cheek, lifting her face to his blazing gaze. "Sweetheart, what is it?" His piercing, probing inspection found no blatant wound, but he held her gently in fear. "Are you injured? Where? How?"

"Not me," she managed and let her body lean into his. "Shadow."

Ty's head lifted. His hard stare found the beloved burden Tempest carried. The wounds and the blood of the wolf seeping into the coat Merrill should have worn told the story. "The grizzly."

Merrill only shuddered. "Dead."

"Where?"

"Wildflower Canyon." Her lips moved woodenly, her words were a stilted recitation, as if it were something she'd gone over and over again in her mind. Something to keep her going, when a man or woman twice as strong, twice as big, would have collapsed. "Shadow." She turned her face to Tempest, to the limp shape beneath her crimson soaked jacket. "He saved us."

Tynan only had eyes for Merrill. Now that he knew the blood wasn't hers, much as he loved Shadow, his next consideration must be the boy. "Casey? Where is he?" When she seemed not to hear, he said again, each word measured, commanding her attention. "Where is Casey, Merrill? Did he go with you to the canyon?"

"Yes." She nodded and her eyes were glazed and unfocused.

"Tell me where he is."

"He helped get Shadow on Tempest. Then went for Carl on Charley. On Charley, for Carl. For Shadow." She was talking in circles but didn't know.

With Casey gone, she'd walked alone, heaven only knew

how many miles and how many hours. Without a coat, with
a shirt wet with Shadow's blood freezing to her. Worn and
torn moccasins soaking her feet.

"You can let go, now." Ty took Tempest's reins from her
resisting grip. "I'll take care of him."

Bogart was skittish at first with the lingering scent of bear
mingling with coppery taint of blood. But he settled with a
stern word and stood while Ty lifted Merrill onto his back.
Mounting behind her, holding her in his arms as she slumped
against him, leading Tempest, he rode grimly toward the
ranch.

Carl was there, just arriving with Cat and Casey. From the
look of the Jeep, he'd driven cross-country, where no such
vehicle should have been able to go. The older man moved to
Bogart's side, his arms upraised. "Give me your woman. I'll
see to her."

"No!" Ty's voice was harsh and ringing, then softened.
"Take care of Shadow, I'll look after her."

While Carl and Casey took Shadow from Tempest, Ty dis-
mounted. When he would have taken the somnolent Merrill
from Bogart, Cat was there to help. A strong silent woman,
lending her strength, for the woman Carl called his.

Once inside his house and the bedroom that had become
hers, his thoughts as frozen by fear as Merrill's had been by
horror and cold and exhaustion, Ty hardly knew what to do.
Or where to begin.

It was Cat who took charge. "Put her there on the bed,"
she directed. "Then go help Carl and Casey with Shadow.
Leave Merrill to me."

"But she might need me or want me," he protested.

"Yes, she will, without a doubt, but not right now."

"What if she needs a doctor? Do you know how far she
walked, how long she was in the cold, with her coat holding
Shadow together?"

"I know." Cat held on to her composure as she walked Ty
to the door. The last thing any of them needed now was panic.
"If she needs a doctor, we'll call one."

"What if she's bad?"

"Then we'll call a helicopter."

"Cat…"

"Go, Tynan," the tall woman said firmly. "Leave me to do what she needs. Don't you understand she wouldn't want you to see her as she is. Nor as she will be when the pain of thawing tissues starts."

"Why?" He was truly puzzled.

"Because she loves you and would spare you, you silly fool. Which is something all of us but you seems to know."

But he did know. He had for a long time. If there had ever been any doubt of it, she'd swept them away by risking herself to bring his wolf back to him. "I'll go," he heard himself saying. "But you'll call if she needs me?"

"Merrill will call you, when she needs you. Never doubt it," Cat said firmly and shut the door in his face.

The house was quiet again. And for the first time in days, at peace. Once the doctor Tynan insisted must be called for Merrill departed, and Shadow's perilous condition stabilized, Carl and Cat left as well. Casey stayed a day longer, seeing to the livestock while Tynan tended the sleeping wounded.

Carl, who possessed the gift of healing hurt creatures, had warned that the wolf would be virtually comatose while its body replenished its losses. He was adamant that Merrill's quick action contributed as much to Shadow's survival as the refrigerated temperature that slowed and depressed the bleeding and vital signs. With care and rest, and God willing, he predicted Shadow would enjoy a few more good years.

As the days passed and Casey said his goodbyes, Tynan found himself in an eerily quiet house. Alone, yet not alone. With Shadow waking only to lap at the broth Cat had left. And Merrill only to drink a little, eat less, and soak in the tub as if she would never be warm again. Then it was back to sleep for both.

The only interruption of his days was the arrival of rangers and officials come to investigate the killing of one of an endangered species. Just cause was easily established and corroborated by Casey. And the grave eyed men took their questions away without disturbing Merrill.

She slept deeply, the sleep of the exhausted. And, Ty thought, of one who had come to terms with herself, with mind and spirit healing at last.

Though she thrived, her color normal, appetite returning, he could not bring himself to leave her alone in the darkness. His nights were spent sitting in a chair by her bed, watching over her as she slept. The little ease he allowed himself was quite simply when sleep overtook him, there in his chair in the small hours of the morning, demanding rest for a weary body.

He was sleeping, as always by her bedside, when she woke. Finished with the somnolence of healing, ready to accept and face what she must, she called to him softly, waking him gently.

He was instantly alert, surprised only that she was half sitting, half reclining, as she regarded him from her bed. "Merrill, what's wrong?"

"Nothing with me." She shook her head, letting the tousled mass of her hair fall over her shoulder. "But you're another matter." In a shaft of moonlight made more brilliant by a new fall of snow, he was drawn and haggard, with worry etched deeply in the bracketing lines around his mouth and mustache. "What are you doing here?"

"Watching you sleep."

"Watching me? How long?"

Even with a frown drawing fine lines across her face, she had never been more appealing or seductive than in the flannel shirt Cat had found while rummaging in the back of his closet. Declaring it the very thing one should wear while thawing, she had promptly buttoned Merrill into it. The shirt was far too large, and should have dwarfed her. But, worn soft and thin by age and wear, it clung and conformed to the lines and curves of her body. Even as the shoulders drooped to her elbows, the sleeves spilled beyond her fingertips, and the hem brushed her knees. In the days that followed, as she found it most comfortable, it had become ritual that it would be worn and washed, then worn again.

Once the flannel had been darkest green. But, with time and age, had faded to a softer shade, in perfect compliment to her skin. The picture she made, disheveled and vulnerable in something of his, made him ache to touch her. As desire flowed like a wellspring within him, he had to struggle to keep his voice level, his tone composed. "This is the fourth night."

"Shadow?" The sheet that had fallen in a puddle at her waist, crumpled in her fist.

"He sleeps by the fire in the great room, and grows stronger every day. Thanks to you."

"Not just me." Merrill had a vague recollection of Cat and Carl and Casey moving around her. But now the house had the feel of emptiness. She sensed on some level she didn't understand and couldn't explain, that she and Tynan and Shadow were alone.

"You look tired." Letting her gaze range over him, she noted his only concession to his own comfort was a pair of faded sweats he wore when he worked at the computer long into the night. "Have you slept at all?"

"Enough."

"I don't think so." Shaking back her hair, as moonlight struck gold, she lifted her arms. "Come here, Tynan. You've watched over me while I found the peace and rest I needed. Now let me do the same for you."

Ty hesitated, not certain that either of them knew what she was asking. "Merrill." His voice was husky and not nearly as composed as he wished. "You don't understand."

"I'm a woman, Ty, not a child. And I understand. The troubles I brought to *Fini Terre* haven't blinded me to your needs nor to my own. But first things first. You've exhausted yourself for me. All I'm asking is that you allow me the plea- sure of returning some small measure of the same tenderness and compassion."

"Sweetheart, you don't owe me anything. There was never any price tag for..."

"For caring?"

"Yes." *For loving you. For wanting you more than I've ever wanted anyone or anything. For dying a little inside, each time I think of losing you.* "Yes," he said again, putting his thoughts aside. "For caring."

"This isn't payment or any debt. It's something for me, something I need." Her hands dropped to the sheet, her gaze was unwavering, her voice soft in the moonlight. "Four days ago, you came tearing up the trail to me. You took me in your arms. You comforted me and warmed me. What did you feel?"

"Relief." Tynan had sat unmoving, listening. Now he rose from his seat, approaching her bedside. Taking her hand, lacing his fingers through hers, he brushed her knuckles with the pad of his thumb. "As if a great void had been filled, the anguish of it eased."

"Yes," she murmured. Drawing him down to sit at the edge of her bed, she combed a shaggy curl from his forehead. "You're tired." Her fingers slipped from his forehead to his nape, bringing his mouth to hers. Her kiss was light and slow, and more passionate in its tenderness than he'd ever known. "You need to sleep." She didn't speak of anguish, but it was there as she whispered against his lips, "And I need to hold you."

Lying back, she drew his unresisting body to her. Cradling his head on her breast, she stroked his hair and breathed in the seductive male scent of him. "Rest," she crooned in an undertone. "Sleep. Then whatever happens, we'll deal with it. And rejoice."

Tynan's mind drifted. His body relaxed. As her hands and her voice soothed him and caressed him, he slept.

When the moon was setting, he woke. In the first light before the dawn, it seemed natural and right that he make love to her. Once more there was untold passion in tenderness.

Then the rising sun blazed down on them, filling their world with spangled sundust. And as Merrill promised, it was a time of joy.

Nine

It was morning when he woke again. The sun was fully risen and the day well begun. Merrill stood at the window, his open shirt nearly falling from her shoulders as she stared out at the land. The sky was an endless, soul searing blue rising into forever above the relentless silence of winter-clad peaks. A canvas worthy of all of Casey's unique talents, commanding attention and never to be forgotten. Yet she was so deeply riveted in thought he wondered if she saw anything at all.

Sliding from the bed, with the hushed step of bare feet, he went to her. Lacing his fingers at her waist, his palms lying against the naked curve of midriff and abdomen, he drew her back against him. "Good morning." His lips brushed her temple in a kiss as delicate as the sweep of an eyelash. "Did you sleep well?"

Hugging his arms closer to her, Merrill leaned back against his shoulder. "The best I have in years."

"Any regrets?"

"About this? About us?" Turning her head, she kissed the tanned and weathered flesh of his throat. "Never."

"Sure?"

"As sure as I will ever be of anything in my life."

"You were awfully involved in something when I interrupted."

"Just taking stock. Facing the past and the truth as it was, not as I saw it. Making myself recognize that Guiterrez is and was exactly what you said he'd become. Slick, slimy, a monster. Then, admitting that my sin was in being too trusting, too naive, too gullible. And, tragically for those who depended on me, far too easily manipulated." As the litany of her shortcomings grew long, she lifted a shoulder, a tiny expression of great contempt. "Everything it was my job not to be. Making me Guiterrez's puppet and his dupe."

"As I was," Ty reminded, with no trace of past bitterness malingering.

"You were blinded by an old friendship."

"All the more reason to see the change in him." He would allow himself no more excuse than she. Yet, perhaps he could now, judging himself in light of another. For another. "We weren't the first he'd fooled and we won't be the last. Ramon Guiterrez is a master at creating illusions, at letting people see in him what they think he is. Even what they want him to be.

"There have been others like him, and others like us. There will be again. Despots, tyrants, misogynists. All of them monsters who will use, abuse, and destroy any in their path. Theirs is an endless list, but none will ever be better, or worse, at the game Guiterrez plays."

Merrill shivered, and was grateful for the solace of his embrace. "The innocents, the women, old and young, and even the children were nothing to him. They were a bargaining chip, a ploy, his means to an end. And when he was done with them, useless chaff to be discarded without a care."

Her voice trembled, her throat constricted with the ache of grief, as she spoke the thoughts that had drawn her from her bed. "Mothers and grandmothers, daughters and small sons, all of them doomed from the minute he made them captive.

"I will always mourn them." Her nails scored Ty's arms, but she didn't know. "And, God help me, I'll always wonder if I'd seen through him, used better judgment, made better choices…"

As her voice faded to a broken whisper and then ceased, his cheek lay against her head, his lips touched her forehead. "I would stake my life that you made the best choices you could." A flex of his arms pressed his naked chest closer against her, his grasp tensed as if he fought not to shake her, make her believe. "Remember, murderers couldn't murder if they looked and acted like murderers. Con men couldn't con. Thieves couldn't steal. The perverted couldn't molest. In a perfect world all evil would wear the mark of evil and be locked away on sight."

"And no one would be hurt, ever." Pausing, she sank deeper into his embrace.

Ty held her as the magnificence of an imperfect world sprawled within their sight, and thoughtful silence spun a pensive truth about them.

"In a perfect world," Merrill said wistfully at last. "But ours isn't. And as beautiful as it is, it will never be. There will always be evil, and always the charlatans and the monsters. The pretenders, who will never be what they seem." She turned her head from Ty, her unseeing gaze on the land he called *Fini Terre*. "Still, if I'd been wiser, if just this once…"

"The world had been a little closer to perfect?" Ty suggested, going where she led.

Merrill closed her eyes, her chin dipped, just once, barely.

"Too much had come before you, sweetheart. Too much had been set into motion. If you possessed all the wisdom of all the sages, nothing would have changed." He was fierce and immutable, even as his voice roughened with anguish. "And, in the end, another name would have been added to the list of those Guiterrez has, and will, destroy in his quest for power."

"Merrill Santiago." She said her own name dispassionately, as if the chance she could have been among those lost was not new.

"Yes! Dammit!" There was no dispassion in Ty. There could never be with the unthinkable. "Merrill Santiago. A name on a gory list, instead of a kind and giving woman, alive, and here in my arms." He rocked her in his embrace, acknowledging completely how meaningless his life would be without her. "I don't think I could bear any sort of world without you."

Merrill sighed softly. "You couldn't miss what you never knew."

"I would know my life was emptier. That the woman who was meant to be mine had never come to me."

"There would have been someone else. Someday."

"No." Ty said no more. A single disputing word making his case far more eloquently than the greatest argument.

Something softened inside her, eased. Brightened. "Then you think this was destined to be? That I was and I am meant for you?"

His lips touched her hair, as he savored the clean scent. "No more and no less than I was meant for you."

"Fate, Mr. O'Hara?"

Turning her in his arms, he lifted her chin with the touch of a finger. "Truth, Miss Santiago."

Rising on tiptoe, she kissed him, letting the taste of him warm her lips. Feeling the steady, assuring beat of his heart against her breast. At the touch of her mouth, his responded, molding, teasing. Taking all she was, all that she offered. Giving back a sweet familiar pleasure. Her pulse leapt, raced, then slowed to a sultry throb. As she drank in the hot and heady sensation, as she reveled in his powerful masculinity, the smoldering desire he had tantalized and taunted so wonderfully wickedly, so maddeningly through the night, burst into sanity destroying tenacity.

When his hands slipped beneath her shirt to stroke and caress her, gliding over her back and her ribs, brushing the sides of her breasts, her sigh was low and hushed. The first and last of soul cleansing tears shimmered in her eyes and on her gold tipped lashes, while his lips moved over hers. An exploration as tender as his caress, stirring mysterious and unnamed sentiments.

"Ty," she whispered softly into his kiss. A name for the mysterious, for the unnamed, for the light in the darkness of her heart.

"Yes, Ty." And even as it cherished, his mouth became a brand, burning deeper, harder. Marking her as his, and himself as hers. He wanted her with consuming desperation. He needed her with the shamelessness of a virile man who believed in his own strength and accepted his needs. And from this day forward, he knew with the surety of his strength and the power of his need, he would never be complete without her.

Shaken, needing to think, to regain some sense of order and balance and truth, he lifted his mouth from the sweet enticement of hers. Yet in the small separation, he discovered there was no order, no balance, no truth, except that which she'd brought to his life. "Merrill..."

"No." Her lips sealed his, stopping the words she wanted to hear, wanted to say. When she moved away only enough to look at him, her gaze was radiant and unwavering. "One day we'll both say what's in our hearts."

Searching her face, Ty saw only tenderness. "One day," he promised and let his hands fall from her, giving her space. "But not yet."

Reaching out to him, with her fingertips she traced the line and contour of his face as if she were memorizing it. Lingering at the chiseled line of his cheek and the tilt of his mustache, finding the pulse beneath his jaw, then in the hollow of his throat. Her quest came to an end against the solid support of his chest and the thundering rhythm of his heart.

"I have to go back, you know."

Ty bowed his head, but didn't speak. In the intensity of the moment he'd let himself forget, but he knew. He'd known for a long while, perhaps even before Merrill, that one day she would go back to her own world. That she must, at least for a while.

"When you hold me, I can face anything, and see everything as it should be. Guiterrez, the children, myself. But I have to stand on my own. I have to trust my judgment, with or without you. The unexpected rapport with Casey was a beginning. Watching him mend and grow and reach out, added confidence as well. But dealing with the grizzly in Wildflower Canyon was a step in the direction I must go."

"Acting as the situation demanded." If he shut his eyes, Ty could see the bear, humpbacked, silvertipped and grizzled. One of two with half a front paw missing. And for the maiming loss, that much more unpredictable. That much more dangerous. In his mind's eye he saw it, a thousand pounds of crazed, killing fury threatening Casey. And Merrill, a feather in comparison, challenging the beast, acting, reacting. Coolly, competently. Effectively. "With the instinct that leaves no room for doubt or hesitation. When either would be fatal."

"Instinct without doubt." Merrill mulled over the clear cut analysis that came so naturally to Ty. "Yes! Exactly the reactions I couldn't be sure I would have. Or ever will again."

"It's important that you do?" A question that needed no answer, for it was written on her face.

"More than important. Necessary."

"Why?" Ty wanted this, at least.

Merrill's eyes were bright. Golden brown, glittering with flecks of amber, in a look that was unwavering. "To be the woman Tynan O'Hara deserves."

"Tynan O'Hara's woman." He liked the sound of it. The intent.

"The last thing I remembered for days after Wildflower Canyon, was Carl calling me that—your woman." She said it reverently, as one might declaring oneself queen or saint. "I don't remember when he said it, or where. Yet his voice seemed to reach out to me through a suffocating mist. And it seemed right."

"If?" Ty let the thought hang, waiting for Merrill to complete it as he knew she would.

"If I can come to you whole. If I can live in your world, not hide in it. If I can stand at your side, not lean."

"To do that you must lay your doubts to rest? Your doubts," he spoke with emphasis. "Not mine."

Taking his hand, she clasped it in both of hers. "You make it hard to go."

"I would make everything in your life easier if I could. Except leaving me." He gripped the hands that held his tightly. "But, I understand, and accept your decision. I won't try to stop you."

Merrill lifted their joined hands to her cheek, her lips were soft and tender against his wrist. "Thank you for that, and for your trust."

"When?" The question was strained. A stranger's voice, and yet his own. "When will you go."

"Soon." Releasing his hand, lifting her arms to lace her fingers at the nape of his neck, she rose again on tiptoe. Heedless that the shirt she wore swung open, or perhaps glad of it, she let the tips of her breasts caress his chest. "But there's time."

Her body moved and turned, rocking gently against the bareness of his. "Time enough to say goodbye." The line of her body teased his. Enticed. Seduced. "Time enough."

"Time for this." His mouth came down on hers, silencing her. Silencing himself. And she felt his desire, subtle no longer, waiting no longer. Commanding, demanding, as a rage. She was swept from her feet, held fast by arms with the tensile power of steel bands. The room reeled in a kaleidoscope of light and shadow as he took her to a bed still tumbled from a night of love.

Remembering her trembling sweetness, the exquisite delight he found in her, he held her close, his shuddering pulse an uneven cadence. A look of molten blue turned to scorch her with the heat of his desire. "Is this what you want? What you meant to provoke? Passion and lust, and wanting until it becomes a mindless demon.

"Would you have me mindless, my love? Without reason or tenderness." Though he spoke with a quiet gentleness, his hands were curling claws of forceful power at her ribs and her thigh. And though his voice was low, thoughtful, his face was drawn in grim lines of constraint by the battle he waged with himself. "Did you mean this?"

"Yes." She had wanted him to want her in the deepest, most elemental way. Savagely and primitively, without restraint. And yes, a demon rode him, one she had taunted, and she wanted that part of him as well. "And yes, again."

A palm cupped the angle of his throat, petting it lightly as her fingers moved to twist in his hair, bringing his mouth back to her. "I want all of you. The dreamy, mystical magic of your tenderness. The thunder and lightning of the storm within you. I want all that you are for my own."

For the space of a faltering heartbeat, he held himself aloof. But undaunted, as she teased her mouth over his, her tongue darted over the unyielding flesh with lazy lightning of its own.

"Witch," he groaned against her enchanting mouth, and the storm broke, sweeping away the last shred of restraint and reason. His massive shoulders shook and even as he let her body slide down the length of his, even as her toes touched the floor, he was bearing her down. Down to her bed.

His body was long and lean over hers as his kiss devoured her. His hands were hard and wild, and the taste of him lay spicy on her tongue as the last of tenderness fled.

The civilized Tynan O'Hara ceased to exist. There was only the elemental, primitive man and the woman who desired him.

Tangled and forbidden by the flow of his own shirt, he cursed once. Then laughed as he ripped it from her and flung it away. Soon there would be thousands of miles between them. But for now, as the morning sun streamed toward the mountains, there would be nothing.

Then he was driving into her, even as she was reaching for

his shoulders, clutching at him, drawing him deeper and harder to her.

If one was lightning, the other was thunder. One following the other, matching the other, while the fury of their storm mounted. As she opened to him, keeping nothing of herself from him, he rode her slowly, fiercely. Hot blue eyes watching with savage arrogance as each cry shuddered from her and her body convulsed with each new sensation.

Blood burning through him like lava, with his one conscious thought, he searched deeply within himself, finding a final shred of control. Using it, reining in the threatening, cresting urgency, he took her deeper into the void. Close and ever closer to the tortuous splendor.

As she cried out her passion, as her nails scored his back and his shoulders in its demand, as her eyes grew dazed with the first of its pleasure, he bent to kiss her. With his kiss consuming her, he lunged once more, and her body fused in exquisite release with his.

The storm faded, passion ebbed. The room was quiet. Precious minutes ticked away.

Spent, drifting in the remembered ecstasy of lovemaking, they lay entwined. His arms around her, her head on his shoulder, their bodies curled with a naturalness one into the other. The day grew older, brighter, filling the window with its glare.

If he thought about it, Ty could guess the hour within a few minutes. But he didn't want to think about it. He didn't want to guess. Time had become the enemy. For time would take her from him. He wondered if she felt the same.

Skimming a hand over her bare hip, he drew her snug against him. "What are you thinking?"

Her answer was lazy, and languorous, and totally unexpected. "Turkeys."

For a stunned second he was taken aback. Then he began to laugh. Husky and deep, the sound of it ringing through the room. "If that doesn't bring a man back down to earth, I don't know what would. Here I was, thinking you were savoring the miracle we've shared, and maybe thanking your lucky stars

for such a splendid lover, and instead, you're thinking of turkeys?"

Sliding her body over his, she folded her hands on his bare
chest and propped her chin on her thumbs as she regarded him
solemnly. "I was."

"You were?" There was laughter in his look. "What?"

"Savoring the miracle and thanking everything in the uni-
verse for you."

"While you thought of turkeys."

"Well, yes." She drew the admission out as she grinned.
"I was wondering if you had any. Turkeys, I mean, in that
great freezer in the pantry."

"There are a few." His fingers danced up her ribs, tanta-
lizing the fullness of her breasts as they flowed over his chest.
"Would you like to tell me why you're interested?"

"Thanksgiving." Determined to pursue this course of conversation at least a while longer, she clamped her teeth against
a moan as he found new places to explore.

"Last time I looked at the calendar, it was a week away."

"Would you mind if I made Thanksgiving dinner for the
Carlsens, and for you? No!" She corrected almost immedi-
ately. "Brunch. Let's make a day of it."

Ty sobered, a roguish grin vanished. "A day of farewell?"

Merrill's smile slipped as well. A sweep of her lashes veiled
the sudden pain she felt.

"Then we have a week." Stroking a fingertip over the fragile curve of an eyelid, he waited for her to look at him. Meeting her gaze, keeping it, he asked solemnly, "How should we
spend it?"

"Like this." Her lips left a trail of kisses over his chest,
his throat, his chin, then his mouth. When his arms closed
around her, lifting her to him, she whispered, "Every precious
second of it."

"A Thanksgiving toast." Carl tapped his glass. One of Tynan's best, for his best vintage, both brought out of storage
on this festive occasion. "To a fine bird." Raising the glass

he bowed to Merrill. "And to the lady who prepared it, with our thanks for all she's given us. For saving Casey and bringing Shadow back to us."

The turkey was only a skeleton, stripped bare by the ravenous appetites the guests and host had brought to the table. And in Merrill's judgment, it was Shadow who had saved Casey and herself by buying time with his courage and devotion. Giving her the chance to do what she had to. But for Shadow, thin and frail from his ordeal, and sleeping soundly at her feet, she accepted the compliment in the happy spirit in which it had been given.

Throughout the day there had been times when the festive air had grown forced. Then others in which the deep bonds of camaraderie and friendship overshadowed the eminent departure. Only Casey questioned her reasons for going and asked why.

"It's just something I have to do," Merrill told him later, as she knelt to tend the fire while Cat helped Tynan clear the table, and Carl stamped across the snow covered porch to replenish the wood box.

"Is it because of the trouble to the east?" Casey's face was solemn, the eyes that were as arresting as his mother's were grave and steady. "You aren't going over to the part of the state where those crazy cult folks are keeping people hostage, and taking potshots at everyone else, are you?"

"Certainly, I'm not." Merrill was more than a little startled by the questions. Standing in her stocking feet, she had to look up at him. "But why would you think I might?"

"It doesn't take a genius to know you do secret stuff. Dangerous, secret stuff."

"Casey! Where did you get such an idea?"

The look the young boy gave her was pure disgust. "Like I said, it doesn't take a genius. You work with Ty's sister, Val. Mom says she twisted his arm over the telephone and persuaded him to give you a place to rest and recuperate. Val does secret stuff for somebody called Simon. I know, because when I was little, when they didn't know I was around, I heard

Ty telling my mom he was worried about the danger this Simon put her in.''

A frown marred the clear, unlined face. The bright stare was level, accusing. ''Do you work for Simon? Will he send you someplace dangerous?''

Merrill saw no reason to deny what Casey already knew. ''Valentina is, or was, part of HRT. Hostage Rescue Teams,'' she interpreted. ''Her field of expertise is firearms. Mine is languages, and like Val, I work for a man called Simon. But, face it, the only way someone in languages could get into trouble is by talking too much.''

Reaching out, she ruffled his dark hair affectionately. ''Hey, buddy, are you trying to tell me I'm a chatterbox?''

Dodging away from her for the first time ever, his unrelenting frown remained intact. ''You don't come to someplace like *Fini Terre* to recuperate from talking too much.''

Sighing, Merrill set the fire tools aside. ''Okay, the truth. Straight out, with no dodges, no frills. And it doesn't leave this room.''

Again a look of utter, teenage disgust flashed over Casey's face, letting her know he understood she might tell him the truth, but there would be no great revelation of national secrets.

Crossing her arms as if she were chilled, even though the fire blazed with renewed vigor, Merrill gave him a capsule version of the truth. ''I was sent on a mission in South America. As usual it was intended that I would be first in, first out. There were some liaisons to be arranged, then some decision to be made. The sort I've made hundreds of times before. Except this time I was wrong.'' She hugged herself closely, never looking away from Casey. ''Some people died. I had a hard time dealing with my part in it.''

''Somebody tricked you,'' Casey said with the candor of youth.

''That's about the size of it.''

''So Valentina sent you to Ty. And now that he's helped you get better, you want a crack at South America again. To make it right, so what happened to those people won't happen to any others."

"You're batting a thousand, champ."

Casey nodded, absently, and Merrill wondered if he'd even heard her until he straightened from the mantel. "Makes sense. It's what I would want." He towered over her, long, lanky, but with the breadth of shoulders that would someday rival his father's. "But you gotta promise you'll be careful. And that you'll come back."

"I promise, I'll be careful." A muffled sound caught Merrill's attention. As she looked past Casey, she found Ty, watching and waiting. A small wistful smile tilted her lips and crinkled her eyes. "And I'll be back. Count on it."

The rest of the morning went quickly. Too quickly for Merrill, though it was barely noon when they gathered closely in the great room. Cat and Casey worked a puzzle that seemed to be nothing but jellybeans. While Carl and Ty discussed horses, and once the grizzly as they speculated on the odds that there would be two bears with the same maiming injury in the same area.

"In a way, it seems far-fetched, stretching the realm of credibility. Then again, where there are poachers there are forgotten and neglected traps. Who's to say more than one bear didn't step into more than one trap." Carl's voice turned harsh. "Some of these steel brutes I've found, could snap half a paw, or even a whole foot off."

From her place on the floor by the fire, with Shadow's head in her lap, Merrill watched, and listened without hearing. I'll be gone tomorrow, she thought with a heavy heart. And who knows when I'll see them again.

As if he read her mind, Ty paused in the conversation, smiled at her and reached down to take her hand. His fingers laced through hers, he turned back to Carl. "I'm going to have the guides and cowhands come a little early next season. Do a careful search."

"Then you think there are more? And you're worried that

some of the summer people will be injured?'' Cat laid aside
another piece of the puzzle as she turned from the blinding
intricacies of thousands of identical jellybeans.

"I'm lucky it didn't happen this past season." Ty's jaw
tightened, a muscle twitched. "A trap that can do that to a
bear could snap a small person's leg, through and through. Or
kill a child.''

"So, first we find the traps," Carl snarled in his hatred for
the cruelty and lack of responsibility. "Then we find the son
of an idiot who set them.''

"He could be long gone," Casey suggested. "In fact, if
he's heard what happened here, I'd bet he is.''

"If we don't find him," Carl put in, "at least the word will
get out we're looking. Could deter anyone else from being so
stupid.''

"It's worth a try.''

The shrill ring of the telephone at Casey's elbow cut Ty
short. With the ease of long custom the boy lifted the receiver.

"O'Hara residence. Casey Carlsen speaking." His words
flowed like silk, if there was hesitation, or a slurred consonant,
only one with a perfect ear for diction would know. Drawing
a surprised gasp, Casey listened, his look finding Merrill first,
then moving to Ty. "Yes, sir," he said gruffly into the receiver. "He's here now.

"It's for you." An obvious observation and unsurprising,
until he offered the telephone, adding, "Simon McKinzie calling.''

The room was suddenly a tomb, with the crackle of blazing
wood resounding like gunfire in the stillness.

"Simon, happy Thanksgiving." Ty said into the receiver as
he took it from Casey. "How are..." Paling he let the rest of
his greeting fall away. His mouth drooped down in a thin,
grim line. At last, with a jerk of his head, he said to Simon,
"I'll go. One way or another, I'll do it. I'll leave within the
hour.''

There was more, but Merrill didn't hear, as she felt the claw
of fear and dread deep in the pit of her stomach. She had no

idea what was wrong. But, in Casey's words, it didn't take a genius to know it was trouble. Grave trouble.

The clatter of the receiver hitting the floor as it missed the cradle, electrified an already stunned audience.

"An hour ago a government plane went down only a few miles from here. Since then the weather service has issued a storm warning, a rogue that just cooked up. No rescue planes or helicopters are flying. We're closest to the crash site. Piegan's Ridge." As he said the unofficial name known only to the locals, but notorious among them, Ty looked at Merrill with bleak eyes. "There were three on board. Valentina was one of them."

"Val!" Cat was first to react. "My lord! Why? Was she coming here?"

"Not here," Ty said wearily. "To the Fortress."

This was the title given to the farm the group of radicals had taken for its home.

"They have an escalating hostage condition."

"But she's retired," Merrill blurted. "She's done no more than consult since she and Rafe were married."

"The situation involves a child. A diabetic child without insulin." Ty's mouth quirked beneath his mustache, but there was no humor in the smile. "She was always a soft touch for a child."

Carl was rising, reaching for his coat. "What will we need?"

For a minute Ty couldn't think, then the fog of shock cleared, leaving his thoughts keen and orderly. "We'll be climbing."

"I've done some climbing," Merrill said as she rose from the floor. "Quite a bit, in fact. I'll help gather our supplies."

Ty turned on her almost angrily. "You can't go."

"I can," she refuted gently. "And I am."

"No. I can't be worried about both of you."

Framing his face in her palms, Merrill looked deeply into his anguish. "Then focus on Val. Our paths never crossed in The Watch, and I haven't known her long, but in that little

while she became my friend. I owe my life as it is, to her."
Taking her hands away, she stood straighter, finding a well of
strength and confidence in the face of disaster. "Worry if you
will, about Val, or all of us, but don't ask me not to go."

There was a tense, watchful hush again. Ty stared down at
her, challenging her decision to no avail. Then, as if by its
own volition, his hand lifted, the back of it stoking the delicate
hollow of her cheek. His voice was husky with strain. "All
right, we go. The three of us."

Taking that as her signal, Cat leapt to action. "I'll make a
quick call to Rob Patten, then have him make others. Those
who can make it, I'll have him send to base camp at Piegan.
Those who can't, I'll ask to meet at the house. The ridge is
closer to The Triple C. Casey and I will set up a triage and
first aid station there. God willing, with a miracle we won't
need it. But we'll be ready."

Ty and Merrill had scattered to see to the clothing that
would be needed and Casey had shrugged into his coat and
was bringing Cat's as she finished her call. Taking it from
him, she looked to Carl. "Take care, my love. And bring Valentina back to us safely."

Carl's gaze held hers long and calmly, a look filled with all
the words of love she wanted to hear. Touching his lips to her
forehead, he managed a smile. The smile that had stolen her
heart so many years before. "I'll do the best I can."

In a whirl of hats and coats and boots, gathering Casey as
she went, Cat left him. Before her fear for all of them spilled
out.

The plane had been down an hour. It would take another
hour to organize the supplies the trek would require. Then God
alone knew how long the journey to the ridge would take.
They would be racing the storm and the clock. The survivors,
if there were survivors, could be frozen before the rescue party
reached them.

Piegan's Ridge was a devil, and no place to be in the dark
with the best of weather. In the coming storm, a rogue and
the worst sort, it could be a killer.

* * *

The trail up Piegan's Ridge was rough and narrow and slick, when they began the ride. The going was slow and would be slower. Though it was little consolation, they were well ahead of the pace they'd anticipated. Part was due to the fact there were three of them planning and preparing. And more than once, Ty found himself marveling at some critical point Merrill made.

It was she who suggested that one of them go ahead on the smaller and faster snowmobile. In case some survivor stumbled on the trail down and was able to negotiate it.

An unlikely prospect they agreed, but no one wanted to risk losing a poor soul brave enough to try. Carl volunteered to ride point. Packing the machine with as many medical and survival supplies as it would hold, he left the rest to Ty and Merrill.

Working in the cold, they moved quickly, loading the horses in a heated trailer hitched to the Sno-Cat. The tank, as it was affectionately called, looked like nothing so much as a cross between a massive snowmobile and its namesake—a tank. By the time Ty and Merrill climbed into its cab, Carl had been away the better part of an hour.

The way the tank must take was less direct, with narrow passages to be bypassed. Carl had base camp set up and ready for their supplies by the time the heavy machine rumbled over the last hill.

"We have survivors. Or at least one." He greeted them with the news before either of them left the cab. "Someone able to start a fire and savvy enough to know what to burn and how. Smelled their smoke, saw the blaze. A campfire. Maybe luck is running with us. From the position of the smoke, the plane went down in a level clearing near the trail. Barring a slide since summer, we can take the horses the whole way."

Neither questioned Carl's assessment, for he was, himself, savvy enough to know the difference in a deliberate fire and a smoldering, burning aircraft. And only Ty knew the trails better.

"Val," Ty muttered. "She would build a fire."

Later it was with hope in his heart, that he led the way to the trail. And as they followed, neither Merrill nor Carl had suggested that anyone on board would have and could have made the fire.

"Careful," Ty called over his shoulder. "Ice."

The rogue storm had not hit, but the wind was rising and the temperature dropping. Earlier snowstorms had scoured their passage, leaving it like glass for great expanses. Except for these sporadic warnings, Merrill simply put her trust in Tempest and let the mare pick her own path.

Carl rode last. On guard and ready, should either of them slip.

There was no conversation beyond the warnings. With faces and mouths buried deeply in their wrappings, and in the keening of the wind, if any had been inclined, conversation would have been impossible.

The afternoon was in its decline, and the light fading, as they made the last narrow turn that led to the small clearing and the wreckage strewn over it.

"Holy Mother of God." Carl murmured his shocked prayer for there was little left of the small craft. Nothing was recognizable. It seemed impossible that anyone could have survived a crash that reduced every part of the plane to jagged sheets of metal. A manic Paul Bunyan with a can opener couldn't have destroyed it more completely.

"How the hell..." Ty's voice broke even as it was snatched away by the wind. "Who..." He couldn't believe anyone could walk or crawl away from the chaos. Yet, the small fire still burned.

Dismounting, hardly aware that Merrill had come to stand by his side, he looked about, trying to make some sense of it. Searching for his sister.

The stench of fuel was heavy even in the wind. And beneath it, for those who knew it, the taint of blood.

"Val." His cry was ragged, as he stood frozen in place.

They had been in the clearing only seconds, but it seemed hours that his mind had moved like sludge not knowing where to go, what to do.

"Val," he whispered as a plea, and began to move.

Metal shrieked and rattled in the wind. Impervious to its furor, within the destruction lay the utter stillness of desolation. Nothing human moved. The land was an empty ruin.

Then she was there, a small specter washed in crimson, rising from the ground. "Ty?"

"Val?" His step faltered. "Dear God! Val!"

Then he was running. With Merrill and Carl only a step behind.

Ten

There was music and laughter, and the hushed sound of the sea washing over a distant shore. A cloudless sky stretched unbroken to the silver rimmed horizon. The warm midday sun shone down on formal gardens lush with manicured lawns and clipped boxwoods.

A perfect day and a perfect place for a celebration of friends. But as lovely and perfect as it was, Merrill was restless, a little ill at ease.

She had discovered that following the maze of brick and stone lined walks would lead her to a wild and even lovelier English garden. A marvelous jumble of blooming flowers, untamed shrubs and, occasionally, something that looked suspiciously like weeds. There, in keeping with the ambience of a sunny glen, the immaculate walks gave way to wonderful winding paths. After meandering past *Freedom*, the stunning bronze of a woman setting free a sea hawk, they converged and ended on a narrow strip of shoreline by the estuary.

She was tempted to take that path, to wander the wild garden, and stand on the shore, seeking a moment to solitude. But solitude would have to wait. It wouldn't be in good taste for the guest of honor to disappear.

So, instead, she wandered the fringes of the gathered crowd, hoping no one would notice her mood. As she walked the stone ledge of a small pool, snatches of gossip and conversation drifted to her. Phrases and voices that seemed to rise above the quiet buzz, leaping out at her in jangling notes.

"...walked straight into the maw of the grizzly, shooting from the hip. Carl Carlsen says it was damn fine shooting and brave as hell. Was all that saved his son." Imposing in a tuxedo nearly as old as he, Simon stood in a small group clustered on the veranda shaded by the ancient slate roof of the converted hunting lodge.

"These mullioned doors and windows are wonderful. I can't believe Valentina did most of the restoration herself." This from a woman Merrill only vaguely recognized. One of Simon's staff.

"Guiterrez was deposed. A long, complex assignment, but worth the outcome. We all did our part, but it was Merrill who really brought him down. The amazing thing is there were no casualties." Alexis Charles, her recent partner, talking shop. Blond and pretty, looking more like a fashion model in a gown of rose silk, she was a trained and seasoned member of The Black Watch.

Across the pool, with voices skimming over the water, three more fellow colleagues spoke as candidly. Shielded from them by a small copse of ornamental shrubs, but with no way to turn and no escape, she could only listen, feeling trapped, becoming an unwilling eavesdropper.

"Lord! Can you imagine it? Riding that frozen trail with a blizzard on the way, then packing the injured down in the thick of it!" Another of Simon's staff, a voice she couldn't place.

"I wouldn't be here if she hadn't." Jim Hartwell stared down into his empty wineglass. "None of the three of us would be."

"Amen," Joe Cabiness, pilot of the ill-fated plane, declared fervently. "From the look of the plane none of us should be here in the first place. It's for sure we wouldn't be, if it weren't for Merrill and her team." Tapping his glass, he muttered. "And if I had another glass of wine, I'd drink to that."

As they moved away in consensus, in search of more wine, Merrill plucked a small flower from a marble vase. Tearing the petals from it one by one, she watched them swirl and dip like pale pink snowflakes on the gently rippling surface of the pool. She wished more than ever that she could escape. But these were her peers and a few trusted friends, come to this isolated and picturesque inlet on the Chesapeake Bay at Valentina's request to honor her.

Feeling miserable, a little silly with all the accolades heaped upon her, and a whole lot guilty, she stared grimly into the bright water. As the stem fell to her feet, her fingers fretted restively over each other.

"Try this one." A tanned hand offered a second flower. A strong hand, attached to a wrist encased in the cuff of a white shirt peeking from the sleeve of an impeccably tailored jacket. "If this one doesn't help," the man to whom the hand and wrist belonged, murmured, "then we can always try the whole bouquet."

Turning in a started rustle of her slender skirt, Merrill looked into the face of a stranger.

"I know." One dark brow lifted, his head inclined as if she'd spoken. "It's difficult for a modest woman to stand by listening to everyone around singing her praises, isn't it?" He smiled then, the spare lines of his arresting face softening, eyes like dark emeralds glittering.

There was an air of barbaric elegance about him, with his dark hair tipped with silver at his temples, and his body lean, obviously fit. His voice was deep, quiet, unhurried, but it wasn't difficult to imagine an edge of command in it. Just as it wasn't difficult to imagine that beneath the urbane persona, lurked a man who was civilized only because he chose to be.

Yet for no reason than the smile, Merrill suspected he was capable of wicked mischief and great tenderness all at once.

Startled by the direction of her mind and wondering where such an errant thought had come from, yet beginning to understand why this particular stranger had been included in this necessarily exclusive gathering, she picked up the thread of his conversation. "We've never met, how would you know who I am, or if I were modest or not?"

"One needn't meet you or know you to see your modesty, my dear." His gaze was keen and piercing, yet subtle in his study, missing not one detail. In masculine appreciation with not a shred of flirtation, he noted the turquoise gown that was, indeed, modestly cut, but of a fabric that clung with a will of its own at each sway and turn of her body. Her hair had been swept to her crown in a mass of curls. Golden tendrils tumbled from their binding to drift around her shoulders and throat.

Her life had been difficult, and her work fraught with danger, yet an ethereal innocence endured. And he knew she had no idea how alluring she was. How tempting. How deeply she was loved.

"You were described to me only recently, in great and glowing detail. In fact the describer could speak of nothing else." His lips moved once more in a smile. And Merrill was struck again by a sense of mischief and wickedly, delicious secrets. "Merrill Santiago, I would know you anywhere."

"Whoever this person is, this describer, he or she could be lying," she suggested.

"Never," he drawled, letting his green gaze dwell on hers. "You were described to me as beautiful. I can see for myself that's true, so why should any of the rest not be?"

Merrill rolled the stem of the rose he'd given her between thumb and forefinger. This was certainly the strangest party chatter she'd ever been engaged in. "The rest?"

"Oh, there was more. Much more."

"Ouch."

"Don't worry," he said kindly. "All of it was true."

"You know that for a fact, as well, I suppose." This was becoming a congenial sparring match. And though she would have chosen a different subject matter, Merrill discovered she was enjoying herself.

"That you're compassionate, and dedicated, with the look and courage of a lioness?" Suddenly any trace of teasing and mischief was gone from him. "I know that best of all. More than that, I believe it with all my heart."

"With all your heart," Merrill repeated, wondering again who this enigmatic man could be, and how he would know about her at all. He wasn't Black Watch, that much she knew for certain. Though he definitely had the look, the intriguing manner. One of Simon's associates? Perhaps? A trusted friend? Probably. Whatever the case, whoever and whatever he was, he was direct.

"Absolutely," he began.

"Rafe, darling, I see you've met our guest of honor." Resplendent in beaded vest and flowing skirt, Valentina slipped her hand through the bend of his arm. Vibrant and healthy, with no abiding traces of her ordeal on the ridge, she raised her face to her husband's kiss.

"Actually, my love, since I was delayed, we haven't met." Suspiciously without expression, Rafe Courtenay met Merrill's astonished look as he brought Valentina closer, his hand covering hers. "At least not officially."

"You dog!" Valentina scolded. "You've been teasing her, I can tell."

Rafe chuckled. "Only a little."

"I can imagine." Smoothing the lapel of his jacket simply because she wanted to touch him, Tynan O'Hara's sister smiled Tynan O'Hara's smile at Merrill. "In case you haven't guessed, Merrill, this Cajun creature is my husband. He may look like a brigand, and he teases unmercifully, but he's really quite civilized."

"Most of the time, thanks to you." Turning from Valentina, he added, "And to you, Merrill Santiago. You asked how I could know that you're modest and kind and brave." A knuckle stroked his wife's cheek, lingering briefly at the corner of her mouth. "My proof is here. Without you I wouldn't have this scolding virago."

Merrill felt the blush begin. "I didn't climb Piegan's Ridge alone. Tynan and Carl Carlsen were there as well."

"Of course." Rafe inclined his head graciously. "But that doesn't mean we can't show our appreciation to you."

"Then all went well on your trip?" Valentina addressed her husband, whose absence had been explained to Merrill as inadvertent, due to an important business matter.

"Exactly as planned except for a little turbulence on the way home. Making us late."

"But you're here now, and we can begin." There was mischief and delight in the smile she turned on Merrill. "We have something we hope will interest you."

"Please, no," Merrill protested. "The party is more than enough. I've done nothing to deserve all this. You were there when I needed help, all I did was return the favor."

"Favor!" Val arched a brow at Rafe. "Would you listen? She calls saving my life nothing more than a favor!"

"I didn't mean it like that," Merrill tried to explain.

"Of course you didn't." Valentina took her hand. "But to appease me, particularly since I've waited over five months for this day, come and see. Then decide if you will accept this small token, or not."

Merrill was suddenly contrite. The malaise that had less to do with the celebration than other concerns had made her seem surly and unappreciative. "I'd like to see, and I'm sure what you've chosen for me will be wonderful."

"If I may be as immodest as you are modest." Valentina's eyes were dancing. "I think wonderful is an understatement. So, come, we'll let you decide."

Rafe led the way through the small, milling crowd. Their journey was slow, with many interruptions, but at last, he escorted them across the veranda to the house. The country

French architecture of the exterior was reflected in the interior as well. The main room, with one wall filled with shelves of books and wildlife carvings and another devoted to paintings and memorabilia of the bay and the sea, was a marvel in restoration. A testament to Valentina's talents and skill.

Beneath a towering ceiling and flanked by mullioned windows, a massive fireplace waited to warm chilly evenings. With no glassy eyed trophies to remind of its past, the hunting lodge of another era had become a peaceful haven.

Pausing to take it all in, Merrill let herself absorb and feel, and grow comfortable. "This is beautiful."

"It belonged to one of my grandfathers, a couple of generations back. My mother calls him a pirate. My father, renouncing any glamour, simply opts for robber baron. When it fell into disrepair and none of the rest of the family wanted to be burdened with it, I took it," Valentina explained.

"And made it a home." Some burden Merrill thought as her attention was drawn to a small carving. "The chipmunk sliding on a leaf, it looks like one of Casey's."

"So it does," her hostess murmured noncommittally.

"Merrill," Rafe intervened. "Why don't you sit there on the sofa where the light is good, while I get your booty."

She'd barely settled on the seat he'd indicated, when he was laying a prettily decorated package on her knees. Backing away, as he wrapped his arms around his wife, both awaited judgment of their offering.

Merrill was overcome by the kindness and generosity. Sliding her palms over the package and clutching it to her, she looked up at them. "It's been so long since anyone but Casey has given me a gift." A rare happening when she was the family disappointment. Then never after she broke with family tradition. "I'm afraid I've forgotten how to be gracious in receiving."

"Oh, hush!" Valentina, who knew her history and the tragedy of it, was on the verge of tenderhearted tears. "Just open it."

"Yes, ma'am," Merrill said with a small smile and began to tear the paper from the thin, flat package. Except it wasn't a package. When the last sticky bit of tape was dispensed with, and the last fluttering ribbon tossed away, she held a book. A book of photographs.

"Tynan's photographs."

"You were expecting Ansel Adams?" Another quip from Valentina to hide the threatening spill of emotions.

"Memories of Montana." And beneath it in smaller script, *"Fini Terre, A Journey's End."* Merrill traced the graceful calligraphy of the title, deeply embedded in a costly leather binding that bore the imprint of a distinguished publishing house. Then opening it as if it held the treasure of her world, she paged slowly and carefully through it.

Though others had been added, the first were in the order she'd chosen on those quiet evenings of a Montana winter. Each picture was vibrant, each evocative, each with a small caption. And in each she could hear Tynan, speaking of the land he loved.

"It's marvelous," she whispered. A woefully inadequate description, but the best her reeling mind and aching heart could manage.

"Then you like it?" This from Rafe, whose expression was as touched as his wife's.

"How could I not?" Merrill gripped the book as if she would never let it go.

"And the dedication?"

Paging to the front of the book, Merrill looked up at Val, a puzzled frown on her face. "There isn't one."

The woman with Ty's eyes and Ty's smile said gently. "Try the last page."

The last page was a photograph. One Merrill had never seen before and had no idea it had been taken. She stood in profile, pensive and bittersweet. Tempest's reins were in her hand, Shadow lay at her feet. And in the background the stark and magnificent mountains surrounding *Fini Terre* rose to touch the sky.

She remembered that time. The last ride on the mare that had taken her safely to Piegan's Ridge and back again. Her last day with Ty.

The caption was a simple dedication.

"Merrill," she read aloud. "For whom this book was created, in the hope…"

As her voice failed, another began. A familiar voice, a voice much loved. "In the hope that one day she will come back to us. To Montana. To *Fini Terre*. To me."

The precious book tumbled to the floor. She was turning, seeking. First she saw Shadow, his coat rich and dark and healthy. His blue eyes blazing, a wolf's grin on his face.

Then Ty.

Eyes as blue and blazing as Shadow's. And more handsome than she had ever seen him in formal Western attire.

Neither was aware when the Courtenays made their quiet exit. Nor of the music and laughter that was the celebration of a woman's courage.

"You were Rafe's business trip." She blurted the only coherent thought that came to mind.

"You've been back from South America two weeks. I waited. When you didn't come to me, I decided it was time I came to you. You've proven what you set out to prove. It's time to come back to Montana, sweetheart."

Her last doubt crumbled away. The nagging fear that what Tynan felt for her was only a temporary dream vanished. The restlessness within her eased.

A smile tilted one corner of his mouth. "Casey says that if we hurry, he can still show you what Spring is like in Wildflower Canyon."

"I'd like that."

"Then let's go home, Short Bear."

She smiled then, at the silly name, the beloved name. As Tynan always made her smile.

When he opened his arms she flew to him. And in his embrace, the perilous journey of Merrill Santiago came to an end.

There, on the Virginia shore of the Chesapeake, while Shadow danced around them like a puppy, with a kiss and a promise of the love he'd never spoken, he made her forever Tynan O'Hara's woman.

*   *   *   *   *

SILHOUETTE

Desire

COMING NEXT MONTH

THE GROOM CANDIDATE
Cait London

The Tallchiefs & Man of the Month

Thanks to his wild reputation, newlywed Birk Tallchief was still a groom *candidate* to his new bride. Until he lived up to the title of husband, he wasn't reaping any marital rewards with Lacey. So why was Birk still a happy husband?

THE OFFICER AND THE RENEGADE
Helen R. Myers

Hugh Blackstone had been the only man for Taylor Benning...until the court bailiffs escorted him away. Now, fourteen years later, Hugh was free, and Taylor needed to tell him about her son...his son!

THE WOMEN IN JOE SULLIVAN'S LIFE
Marie Ferrarella

Bachelor Joe Sullivan considered himself an expert on women. But little girls? Suddenly, he had three to bring-up and he desperately needed a miracle! Then one turned up—Maggie MacGuire—but why did she prefer the kids' kisses to his?

BOSS LADY AND THE HIRED HAND
Barbara McMahon

Single mum Amanda Williams needed a ranch foreman. But could she trust sexy Hawk Blackstone to save her business and not seduce her?

DR HOLT AND THE TEXAN
Suzannah Davis

Travis King knew his old friend Mercy was off-limits...*if* he wanted to keep his deep, dark secret. Besides, Mercy was the marrying kind and Travis wouldn't abandon his bachelorhood for anyone!

THE BACHELOR NEXT DOOR
Katherine Garbera

When Rafe Santini rescued the single mum next door, Cass Gambrel, he decided he was interested in her—but not in commitment! Still, something about her had him wondering if it was time to end his wandering ways...

COMING NEXT MONTH FROM

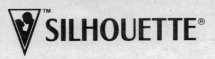 SILHOUETTE®

Sensation
A thrilling mix of passion, adventure and drama

HIDDEN STAR Nora Roberts
THE BACHELOR PARTY Paula Detmer Riggs
MACNAMARA'S WOMAN Alicia Scott
THE TAMING OF REID DONOVAN Marilyn Pappano

Intrigue
Danger, deception and desire

HER DESTINY Aimée Thurlo
RIDE THE THUNDER Patricia Werner
BEFORE THE FALL Patricia Rosemoor
BEN'S WIFE Charlotte Douglas

Special Edition
Satisfying romances packed with emotion

WHITE WOLF Lindsay McKenna
A COWBOY'S TEARS Anne McAllister
THE RANGER AND THE SCHOOLMARM Penny Richards
HUSBAND: BOUGHT AND PAID FOR Laurie Paige
WHO'S THE DADDY? Judy Christenberry
MOUNTAIN MAN Doris Rangel

On sale from July, 1998

LAURA VAN WORMER

❦ ★ ❦

Just for the Summer

Nothing prepares Mary Liz for the summer she spends in
the moneyed town of East Hampton, Long Island. From
the death of one of their own, Mary Liz realises that these
stunningly beautiful people have some of the ugliest
agendas in the world.

*"Van Wormer,...has the glamorama Hampton's scene down to
a T. (Just for the Summer is) as voyeuristic as it is fun."*
— Kirkus Reviews

1-55166-439-9
AVAILABLE FROM JUNE 1998

MIRA®

EMILIE RICHARDS

RUNAWAY

Runaway is the first of an intriguing trilogy.

Krista Jensen is desperate. Desperate enough to pose as a young prostitute and walk the narrow alley ways of New Orleans. So it's with relief that Krista finds herself a protector in the form of Jess Cantrell. Grateful for his help, she isn't sure she can trust him.

Trusting the wrong man could prove fatal.

MIRA®

1-55166-398-8
AVAILABLE FROM JUNE 1998

4 FREE

books and a surprise gift!

We would like to take this opportunity to thank you for reading this Silhouette® book by offering you the chance to take FOUR more specially selected titles from the Desire™ series absolutely FREE! We're also making this offer to introduce you to the benefits of the Reader Service™—

- ★ FREE home delivery
- ★ FREE gifts and competitions
- ★ FREE monthly newsletter
- ★ Books available before they're in the shops
- ★ Exclusive Reader Service discounts

Accepting these FREE books and gift places you under no obligation to buy; you may cancel at any time, even after receiving your free shipment. Simply complete your details below and return the entire page to the address below. *You don't even need a stamp!*

YES! Please send me 4 free Desire books and a surprise gift. I understand that unless you hear from me, I will receive 6 superb new titles every month for just £2.50 each, postage and packing free. I am under no obligation to purchase any books and may cancel my subscription at any time. The free books and gift will be mine to keep in any case.

D8XE

Ms/Mrs/Miss/Mr.................................Initials ....
BLOCK CAPITALS PLEASE

Surname ....

Address ....

....

....Postcode................................

Send this whole page to:
THE READER SERVICE, FREEPOST, CROYDON, CR9 3WZ
(Eire readers please send coupon to: P.O. BOX 4546, DUBLIN 24.)

The Sunday Times **bestselling author**

PENNY JORDAN

TO LOVE, HONOUR &

Motherhood, marriage, obsession, betrayal and family duty... the latest blockbuster from Penny Jordan has it all. Claudia and Garth's marriage is in real trouble when they adopt a baby and Garth realises that the infant is his!

"Women everywhere will find pieces of themselves in Jordan's characters."

—Publishers Weekly

1-55166-396-1
AVAILABLE FROM JULY 1998